THE

SHORT LINE WAR

THE

SHORT LINE WAR

BY

MERWIN–WEBSTER

THE GREGG PRESS / RIDGEWOOD, N. J.

First published in 1899 by The MacMillan Co.
Republished in 1967 by
The Gregg Press Incorporated
171 East Ridgewood Avenue
Ridgewood, New Jersey, U.S.A.

Copyright© 1967 by
The Gregg Press, Inc.

Library of Congress Catalog Card Number: 67-29273

Printed in United States of America

AMERICANS
IN
FICTION

INTRODUCTION BY PROFESSOR CLARENCE GOHDES
Editor of *American Literature* Magazine

In the domain of literature the play may once have been the chief abstract and chronicle of the times, but during the nineteenth and twentieth centuries the novel has usurped the chief place in holding the mirror up to the homely face of society. On this account, if for no other, the Gregg Press series of reprints of American fiction merits the attention of all students of Americana and of librarians interested in building up adequate collections dealing with the social and literary history of the United States. Most of the three score and ten novels or volumes of short stories included in the series enjoyed considerable fame in their day but have been so long out of print as to be virtually unobtainable in the original editions.

Included in the list are works by writers not presently fashionable in critical circles — but nevertheless well known to literary historians — among them Joel Chandler Harris, Harriet Beecher Stowe, Thomas Bailey Aldrich, and William Gilmore Simms. A substantial element in the list consists of authors who are known especially for their graphic portrayal of a particular American setting, such as Gertrude Atherton (California), Arlo Bates (Boston), Alice Brown (New England), Edward Eggleston (Indiana), Mary Wilkins Freeman (New England), Henry B. Fuller (Chicago), Richard M. Johnston (Georgia), James Lane Allen (Kentucky), Mary N. Murfree (Tennessee), and Thomas Nelson Page (Virginia). There is even a novel by Frederic Remington, one of the most popular painters of the Western cowboy and Indian — and another, an impressive minor classic on the early mining region of Colorado, from the pen of Mary Hallock Foote. The professional student of American literature will rejoice in the opportunity afforded by the collection to extend his reading of fiction belonging to what is called the "local-color movement" — a major current in the development of the national belles-lettres.

Among the titles in the series are also a number of famous historical novels. Silas Weir Mitchell's *Hugh Wynne* is one of the best fictional treatments of the American Revolution. John Esten Cooke is the foremost Southern writer of his day who dealt with the Civil War. The two books by Thomas Dixon are among the most famous novels on the Reconstruction Era, with sensational disclosures of the original Ku Klux Klan in action. They supplied the grist for the first great movie "spectacular" — *"The Birth of a Nation"* (1915).

Paul Leicester Ford's *The Honorable Peter Stirling* is justly ranked among the top American novels which portray American politics in action — a subject illuminated by other novelists in the Gregg list — A. H. Lewis, Frances H. Burnett, and Alice Brown, for example. Economic problems are forcefully put before the reader in works by Aldrich, Mrs. Freeman, and John Hay, whose novels illustrate the ominous concern over the early battles between labor and capital. From the sweatshops of Eastern cities in which newly arrived immigrants toiled for pittances, to the Western mining camps where the laborers packed revolvers, the working class of the times enters into various other stories in the Gregg list. The capitalist class, also, comes in for attention, with an account of a struggle for the ownership of a railroad in Samuel Merwin's *The Short-Line War* and with the devastating documentation of the foibles of the newly rich and their wives in the narratives of David Graham Phillips. It was Phillips whose annoying talent for the exposure of abuses led Theodore Roosevelt to put the term "muck-raker" into currency.

While it is apparent that local-color stories, the historical novel, and the economic novel have all been borne in mind in choosing the titles for this important series of reprints, it is evident that careful consideration has also been given to treatments of various minority elements in the American population. The Negro, especially, but also the Indian, the half-breed, Creoles, Cajuns — and even the West Coast Japanese — appear as characters in various of these novels or volumes of short stories and sketches. Joel Chandler Harris's *Free Joe* will open the eyes of readers who know that author solely as the creator of humorous old Uncle Remus. And there is a revelatory volume of dialect tales, written by a Negro author, *The Conjure Woman* by Charles W. Chesnutt.

In literary conventions and the dominating attitudes toward life, the works in the Gregg series range from the adventurous romance illustrated so well by Mayne Reid or the polite urbanity of Owen Wister to the mordant irony of Kate Chopin and the grimmer realism of Joseph Kirkland's own experiences on bloody Civil War battlefields or the depressing display of New York farm life by Harold Frederic. In short, the series admirably illustrates the general qualities of the fiction produced in the United States during the era covered, just as it generously mirrors the geographical regions, the people, and the problems of the times.

CONTENTS

vi   *Contents*

THE SHORT LINE WAR

CHAPTER I

JIM WEEKS

JAMES WEEKS came of a fighting stock.

His great-grandfather, Ashbel Weeks, was born in Connecticut in 1748; he migrated to New York in '70, and settled among the Oneida Indians on the Upper Mohawk. It was the kind of life he was built for; he sniffed at danger like a young horse catching a breath off the meadows. He did not take the war fever until St. Leger came up the valley, when he fought beside Herkimer in the ambush on Oriskany Creek. He joined the army of the North, and remained with it through the long three years that ended at Yorktown; then he married, and returned to his home among the half-civilized Oneidas.

His oldest son, Jonathan, was born in '90. He grew like his father in physique and tem-

perament, and his migrating disposition led him
to Kentucky. The commercial instinct, which
had never appeared in his father, was strong
in him, so that he turned naturally to trading.
He began in a small way, but he succeeded at
it, and amassed what was then considered a
large fortune.

In 1823 he moved to Louisville, and interested himself in promoting the steamboat traffic
on the Ohio and Mississippi rivers.   As the
business developed, Jonathan Weeks's fortune
grew with it.   His only son, who was born in
1815, was sent to Harvard; he spent a very
merry four years there, and a good deal of
money.   He fell in love in the meantime, and
married immediately after his graduation.   Not
many months after his marriage he was killed
by the accidental discharge of a rifle, and,
shortly after this, his widow died in giving
birth to a son.

The care of the child devolved entirely upon
Jonathan, the grandfather.   He assumed it
gladly, even eagerly, and his whole existence
soon centred about the boy, and James — for
so they had named him — became more to him
than his son had ever been.   It grew evident

that he would have the Weeks build, and, by the time he was fifteen, he was as lean, big-boned, awkward a hobbledehoy as the old man could wish. His grandfather's wealth did not spoil him in the least; he was the kind of a boy it would have been difficult to spoil.

He had no fondness for books, but it is to be doubted if that was much of a grief to his grandfather. He was good at mathematics, — he used to work out problems for fun, — and an excellent memory for certain kinds of details enabled him to master geography without difficulty. The great passion of his boyhood was for the big, roaring, pounding steamboats that went down to New Orleans. His ambition, like that of nearly every boy who lived in sight of those packets, was to be a river pilot, and he was nearing his majority before he outgrew it.

He was twenty-two years old when he fell in love with Ethel Harvey. She was nineteen when she came home from the Eastern school where she had spent the past five years, and she burst upon Jim in the first glory of her womanhood. When she had grown an old woman the young girls still envied her beauty, and wondered what it must have been in its first bloom.

Small wonder that Jim fell in love with her ; it was inevitable.

He first saw her, after her return, on a bright June morning as he was strolling down the path from his grandfather's house to the street. She was riding her big bay mare at a smart gallop, but she pulled up short at sight of him, and drawing off a riding gauntlet held out her hand. From that moment Jim loved her. The old man was coming down the path, but seeing them there together, he paused, for they made a striking picture. Her little silk hat sat daintily on her hair, which would be rebellious and fluffy ; the dark green riding habit with its tight sleeves revealed the perfect lines of her lithe figure, which swayed gracefully as the mare pawed and backed and plunged, impatient for the morning gallop. She seemed quite in-different to the protests of the big brute, and talked merrily to Jim, who stood looking up at her in bewildered admiration. At last she shook hands again and rode away, and Jona-than Weeks walked back into the house with a satisfied smile. " They'll do," he said.

It looked as though they would. Through the short happy weeks that followed, Ethel did not ride alone. Together they explored the country lanes or left them for a dash straight across the fields, taking anything that chanced to be in the way. In their impromptu races, which were frequent, Ethel almost always won; for racer though he was, Jim's sorrel found the two hundred and eight pounds he carried too much of a handicap. So the days went by, and though nothing was said about it, they talked to each other, and thought of each other, as lovers do.

But all the while there was growing in Ethel's mind an intuition that something was wrong. She had not an analytical mind, but she became convinced that though she might learn to understand Jim, he could never understand her. It was not only that she was the first woman who had come into his life, though that had much to do with it. But he was a man without much instinct or imagination; he took everything seriously and literally, he could not understand a whim. And when she saw how her pretty feminine inconsistencies puzzled him, and how he failed to understand the whimsical, butterfly fancies she confided to him, she would cry with vexation, and think she hated him; but then the knightly devotion of his big heart would win her back again, and her tears would cease to burn her cheeks, and she would tell herself how unworthy she was of the love of a man like that. But the trouble was still there; Ethel grew sad, and Jim, more than ever, failed to understand. The old man watched, but said nothing.

One evening Jim took her out on the river. It was the summer of '61, when the North was learning how bitter was the task it had to accomplish. Kentucky was disputed ground and feeling ran high there; little else was thought of. Jim had been talking to her for some time on this all-absorbing topic while she sat silent in the stern, her hand trailing in the water. Finally he asked why she was so quiet.

"I think this war is very stupid," she said. "Let's talk about"—here she paused and her eyes followed the big night boat which was churning its way down the river—"about paddle-wheels, or port lights, or something."

Jim said nothing; he had nothing to say. She went on:—

"Don't you think it is tiresome to always mean

what you say? I hate to tell the truth. Anybody can do that."

"I thought," said Jim, "that you believed in sincerity."

"Oh, of course I do," she exclaimed impatiently, and again Jim was silent.

The next day he took her for a drive and it was then that the end came. They had been having a glorious time, for the rapid motion and the bright sunshine had driven away her mood of the night before and she was perfectly happy; Jim was happy in her happiness. The half-broken colts were fairly steady and he let her drive them and turned in his seat so that he could watch her. As he looked at her there, her head erect, her elbows squared, her bright eyes looking straight out ahead, Jim fell deeper than ever in love with her. The colts felt a new and unrestraining hand on the reins, and the pace increased rapidly. Jim noted it.

"You'd better pull up a little," he said. "They'll be getting away from you."

"I love to go this way," she replied, and over the reins she told the colts the same thing, in a language they understood. Suddenly one of them broke, and in a second both were running.

"Pull 'em in," said Jim, sharply. "Here —
give me the reins."

"I can hold them," she protested wilfully.
Then, without hesitation and with perfectly unconscious brutality, Jim tore the reins out of her
hands, and addressed himself to the task of quiet-
ing the horses.

It was not easy, but he was cool and strong,
and the horses knew he was their master; nevertheless it was several minutes before he had
them on their legs again. During that time
neither had spoken; then Jim waited for her to
break the silence. He was somewhat vexed, for
he thought she had deliberately exposed herself
to an unnecessary peril. But she said nothing
and they finished their drive in silence.

At her door he sprang out to help her to
alight, but she ignored his offered aid. Though
she turned away he saw that there were tears in
her eyes.

"Ethel," he said softly, but she faced him in
a flash of anger.

"Don't speak to me. Oh — how I hate you!"

Jim seemed suddenly to grow bigger. "Will
you please tell me if you mean that?" he said
slowly.

"I mean just that," she answered. "I — I hate you." She stood still a moment; then she seemed to choke, and turning, fled into the house.

To Jim's mind that was the end of it. She had told him that she hated him. The fact that there had been a catch in her voice as she said it weighed not at all with him; that was an unknown language. So he took her literally and exactly and went away by himself to think it over.

He was late for dinner that night, and when he came in his grandfather was pacing the dining room. But Jim wasted no words in explanation.

"Grandfather," he said, "I think if you won't need me for a while I'll enlist to-morrow."

"I can get along all right," said the old man, "but I'm sorry you're going."

The older man was looking at the younger one narrowly. Suddenly and bluntly he asked: —

"Is anything the matter with you and Ethel Harvey?"

Jim nodded, and without further invitation or questioning he related the whole incident. "That's all there is to it," he concluded. "The

team had bolted and she wouldn't give me the
reins; so I took them away from her and pulled
in the horses.   There was nothing else to do."

"And then she said she hated you," added
Jonathan, musingly.   "I reckon she hasn't
much sense."

"It ain't that," Jim answered quickly.   "She's
got sense enough.   The trouble with her is she's
too damned plucky."

A few days later he was a private in the
Nineteenth Indiana Volunteers.   He made a
good soldier, for not only did he love danger as
had his great-grandfather before him, but he
had nerves which months of inaction could not
set jangling, and a constitution which hardship
and privation could not undermine.

The keenest delight he had ever known came
with his first experience under fire.   He felt his
breath coming in long deep inhalations; he could
think faster and more clearly than at other times,
and he knew that his hands were steady and his
aim was good.   Somehow it seemed that years
of life were crowded into those few minutes,
and he retired reluctantly when the order came.

His regiment was in the Army of the Poto-
mac, and the story of its waiting and blundering

and magnificent fighting need not be told again in these pages. Jim was one of thousands of brave, intelligent fighters who did not rise to the command of a division or even of a regiment. He was a lieutenant in Company E when the Nineteenth marched down the Emmittsburg Pike, through Gettysburg and out to the ridge beyond, to hold it until reënforcements should come.

They fought there during four long hours, until the thin line of blue could hold no longer, and gray ranks under Ewell and Pender had enveloped both flanks. Then sullenly they came back through the town, still firing defiantly, and cursing the help that had not come. It was during this retreat that Jim was hit, but he did not drop. Somehow — though as in a dream — he kept with his regiment, and it was not until they were rallied in the cemetery on the other side of the town that he pitched forward and lay quite still.

Everybody knows how the Eleventh Corps held the cemetery through the two bloody days that followed. But Jim was unconscious of it all, for he lay on a cot in the Sanitary Commission tent, raving in delirium. And the surgeons and nurses looked at him gravely and wondered with every hour why he did not die.

But, as one of his comrades had said, " it took a lot of pounding to lick Jim Weeks," and in a surprisingly short time he was strong enough to be taken home.

When he first saw his grandfather he was dimly conscious of a change in him, and as he grew stronger and better able to observe closely he became surer of it. Jonathan had been a young old man when Jim went away; now he looked every one of his seventy-three years, and instead of the tireless energy of former times Jim noted a listlessness hard to understand.

One night after both had gone to bed Jim heard his grandfather groping his way down the stairs and out upon the veranda. He listened intently until he heard the creak of the rocking chair, which told him that the old man was visiting again with old friends and old fancies. The slow rhythm lulled Jim into a doze, and then into sleep. He awakened with a start; his pioneer blood made him a light sleeper, and he knew that the old man could not have got upstairs and past his door without waking him. " He must have gone to sleep down there," thought Jim, and rising he went down to the veranda. Jonathan had gone to sleep, but the black cob pipe was clenched between rigid jaws; his sightless eyes were open and seemed to be looking at the stars.

At first Jim felt that sails, helm, and compass had been swept clean away, but he was strong enough to recover his bearings quickly. His grandfather's death marked an end and a beginning, and just as a needle when a magnet is taken away swings unerringly into the line of force of the original magnet, the earth, so Jim's life swung to a new direction. There was no one whose life could direct or influence his, and alone he started on what business men of the next generation knew as his career.

The war had lessened but not destroyed Jonathan's fortune, and it went without reservation to Jim. The times offered golden opportunities to a man with ready money and good business training, and his success was almost inevitable. His life from this time was the logical working out of what he had in him.

He turned naturally to the railroad business, and those who know the history of Western railroads from '65 to '90 will understand what a field it was for a man who was at once fearless and level-headed. The craze for construction and then the equally mad competition did not confuse him, they simply gave him opportunities. When the reaction against the railroads set in, and the Granger movement wrecked nearly all the Western roads, Jim bowed to the inevitable, but he saved himself — no one knew just how — and when the State legislators were over their midsummer madness he was again in the field, and again succeeding.

With the details of these struggles we are not concerned. The " inside " history of many of them will never be known; in almost every case it differs materially from the story which appeared in the papers. Jim became famous and was libelled and flattered, respected and abused, by turns; but always he was feared. He was supposed to be dishonest, and it is true he did not scruple to use his enemies' weapons; but at directors' meetings it was the interest of the stockholders that he fought for.

Men wondered at his success, and over their cigars gravely discussed the reasons for it. Some said it was sheer good luck that turned what he touched to gold, some laid it to his start, and others to his cool, dispassionate strategy. To some extent it was all of these things; but more than anything else he had won as a bulldog does, by hanging on. Often he had beaten better strategists simply by keeping up the fight when by all the rules he was beaten. For as the comrade of long ago had said, "it took a lot of pounding to lick Jim Weeks."

CHAPTER II

IT was Monday morning, September 23d. The telephone bell on the big mahogany desk rang twice before Jim Weeks laid down the sheet of paper he was scrutinizing and picked up the receiver.

"Hello! Oh, that you, Fox? Yes —— Yes. Hold on! Give me that name again. Frederick McNally. Dartmouth Building, did you say? Yes. Thank you. Good-by."

The bell tinkled again and Jim swung round in his chair.

There was another desk in the room, where sat a young man busy over a pile of letters. He was private secretary to a man who was president of one railroad and director in others, and his life was not easy. The letters he was working over were with one exception addressed to the Hon. James Weeks, Washington Building, Chicago. The exception was a pale blue

16

note addressed to Mr. Harvey West, and the young man had put that at the bottom of the pile and was working down to it.

The elder man spoke. "West," he said, "Fox has just telephoned me that he's found out who's been buying M. & T. stock. It's Frederick McNally; he's in the Dartmouth Building. He isn't doing it on his own hook, but I don't know who he is doing it for. Somebody wants that stock mighty bad. There isn't a great deal of it lying around, though."

"Do you think that Thompson——" began the secretary.

"Thompson would be glad to see me out and himself in," said Jim Weeks, "and he leads Wing and Powers around by the nose, but he can't swing enough stock to hurt anything at next election. I don't believe it's he that's buying. Thompson hasn't got sand enough for that. He'll never fight."

There was a moment's pause. Jim walked over to the ticker and looked back along the ribbon of paper. "It's quoted at 68½ this morning," he said, "but no sales to amount to anything."

"You might go over and talk to Wing," he

c

went on. "You can find out anything he knows if you go at it right. I don't believe there's anything there. However, I'd like to know just what they are doing. You'd better do it now. Send Pease in when you go out, will you?"

Harvey slipped the blue envelope from the bottom of the pile of letters, called the stenographer, and started out. He read the note while he was waiting for the elevator.

The M. & T. is a local single-track road, about two hundred miles long, running between the cities of Manchester and Truesdale. The former is on the main line of the Northern, and the latter on the C. & S. C., both of which are trunk lines from Chicago to the West. The M. & T. was not a money-making affair; it had cost a lot of money, its stock was away down, and it trembled on the brink of insolvency until Jim Weeks took hold of it. He put money into it, straightened out its tangled affairs, and incidentally made some enemies in the board of directors. There were coal mines on the line near Sawyerville, which were operated in a desultory way, but they never amounted to much until some more of Jim Weeks's money went

into them, and then they began to pay. This
made the M. & T. important, especially to the
C. & S. C. people, who immediately tried to
make arrangements with Jim for the absorption
of the M. & T. by their line.   C. & S. C. had a
bad name.   There were many shady operations
associated with its management, and Jim decided to have as little to do with it as possible,
so the attempt apparently was abandoned.

The stock of the M. & T. was held largely
by men who lived along the line of the road.
Tillman City and St. Johns each held large
blocks; they had got a special act of legislature to allow them to subscribe for it.   These
stockholders had great confidence in Jim, for
under his management their investment was
beginning to pay, and they, he felt sure, ap-
proved of his action in the C. & S. C. matter.

Everything was going well with the road,
and the stock was climbing slowly but steadily.
It was not liable to any great fluctuation, for
most of its holders regarded it as a permanent
investment and it did not change hands to any
great extent.   Comparatively little of it got
into the hands of speculators.

But suddenly it began to jump.   It was evi-

dent to every one who watched it that some
important deal was afoot. Jim Weeks was as
much in the dark as any one. He had watched
its violent fluctuations for a week while he
vainly sought to ferret out the motive that was
causing them. And on this particular morning, though he sent his secretary, Harvey West,
to talk to Wing, he had little idea that the
young fellow would get hold of a clew.

When the elevator stopped at the main floor,
Harvey thrust the half-read note back into his
pocket. "No time for that sort of thing this
morning," he thought. "I wonder how soon I'll
be able to run down to see her." A moment later
he was walking rapidly toward the Dartmouth.

The men he saw and nodded to glanced round
at him enviously. "Case of luck," growled
somebody. That was true. Harvey was lucky;
lucky first and foremost in that Ethel Harvey
was his mother. He got his mental agility as
well as his indomitable cheeriness from her.
He was a healthy, sane young fellow who
found it easy to work hard, who could loaf most
enjoyably when loafing was in order, and who
had the knack of seeing the humorous side of
a trying situation. He had always had plenty

of money, but that was not the reason he got
more fun out of his four years in college than
any other man in his class. He "got down to
business" very quickly after his graduation,
and now at the end of another four years he
was private secretary to Jim Weeks. That of
course wasn't luck. The fact that Jim had
fallen in love with Ethel Harvey thirty years
before might account for his friendly interest
in her son, but it would not explain Harvey's
position of trust. He knew that he could not
hold it a day except by continuing to be the
most available man for the place.

It is probable that on this morning, the
contents of the pale blue note contributed
largely to his cheerfulness. It was evident
that Miss Porter liked him, and Harvey liked
to be liked.

Wing's office on the sixth floor of the Dartmouth was a beautifully furnished suite, presided over by a boy in cut-steel buttons. Wing
himself was a dapper little man, a capitalist by
necessity only, for his money had been left to
him. His one ambition was to collect all the
literature in all languages on the game of
chess; a game by the way which he himself

did not play. " Mr. Wing had gone out to
lunch about an hour before," said the boy in
buttons. "Would Mr. West wait?" Harvey,
who knew Mr. Wing's luncheons of old, said
no, but he would call again in the afternoon.
As he walked back to the elevator his eye
fell upon another office door which bore the
freshly painted legend, "Frederick McNally,
Attorney-at-law."

Harvey lunched at the Café Lyon, which is
across the street from the main entrance to
the Dartmouth. The day was warm for late
September, and he selected a seat just inside
the open door. From his table he could see
people hurrying in and out of the big office
building. He watched the crowd idly as he
waited for his lunch, and finally his interest
shifted to the big doors, which seemed to have
something human about them, as they mali-
ciously tried to catch the little messenger boys
who rushed between them as they swung.

Suddenly his attention came back to the
crowd, centring on a party of four men who
turned into the great entrance. Three of them
he knew, and the fact that they were together
suggested startling possibilities. They were

Wing, Thompson and William C. Porter of Chicago and Truesdale, First Vice-President of the C. & S. C. and, this was the way Harvey thought of him, father of the Miss Katherine Porter whose name was at the bottom of the note in the blue envelope. Thompson, a fat, flaccid man with a colorless beard, was laboriously holding the door open for Mr. Porter, then he preceded little Mr. Wing. The fourth man was a stranger to Harvey.

He was starting to follow them when the waiter came up with his order. That made him pause, and a moment's reflection convinced him that he had better wait. He decided that if the meeting of Porter with the two M. & T. directors were not accidental they would be likely to be in consultation for some time, and he would gain more by inquiring for Mr. Wing at the expiration of a half hour than by doing it now. So he lunched at leisure and then went back to the sixth floor of the Dartmouth.

He was met by a rebuff from Buttons. "No, Mr. Wing had not come back yet," and again "Would Mr. West wait?" Harvey could think of nothing better to do, so he sat down to think the matter out. He was puzzled, for the three

men were in the building, he felt sure.   Then it
came to him.   " Jove," he murmured, " Mc-
Nally! McNally was that fourth man."   He
sat back in his chair and tried to decide what
to do.

Meanwhile four men sat about the square
polished table in Mr. McNally's new office and
anxiously discussed ways and means.   The
scrappy memoranda and what appeared to be
problems in addition and subtraction littered
about, made it appear that some ground had
been pretty thoroughly gone over.   There was
a momentary lull in the conversation, and the
silence was broken only by the tapping of Mr.
Wing's pencil as he balanced it between his
fingers and let the point rebound on the top of
the table.   There really seemed to be nothing
to say.   The alliance between C. & S. C. and
Thompson's faction of the M. & T. directors had
been arranged some days before.   They had
met to-day to see how they stood.   McNally
told what he had done, and it was not so much
as they had hoped he would be able to do.
The combination was not yet strong enough to
take the field.   For the past twenty minutes
Thompson had been leaning over the table mak-

ing suggestions in his thick voice, and McNally had sat back and quietly annihilated them by demonstrating their impracticability, or by stating that they had been unsuccessfully tried.

Beyond asking one or two incisive questions of McNally, Porter had said nothing, but had stared straight out of the window. For the past ten minutes he had been waiting for Thompson to run down. It was he who broke the silence.

"We're stuck fast" — he was speaking very slowly — "unless we can get control of that Tillman City stock."

McNally shook his head doubtfully. "I'm afraid it's no good," he said. "Look what we've offered them already. They think the stock is going to go on booming clear up to the sky, and they won't sell. We couldn't get it at par."

Porter's chair shot back suddenly. He walked over to the empty fireplace, the other men watching him curiously. He spread his hands behind him mechanically as if to warm them. Then he said : —

"I think we could get it if we were to offer par."

"Offer par!" thundered Thompson. "We could get Jim Weeks's holdings by paying par."

Porter smiled indulgently. "I didn't say we'd *pay* par for anything. But I think if Mr. McNally were to sign a contract to pay par the day after the M. and T. election, that he could vote the stock on election day."

McNally's plump hand came down softly on the table. "Good!" he said under his breath.

But Mr. Thompson failed to understand. "But the contract?" he said.

"Such a contract would be a little less valuable than that waste paper," Porter replied politely, indicating the crumpled sheets on the table. Then he turned to McNally and asked, "How many men will it take to swing it?"

"Three, if we get the right ones. Yes, I know the men we want. I can get them all right," he added, in response to the unspoken question. "It will need a little — oil, though, for the wheels."

"I suppose so," said Porter, dryly. "I think you'd better get at it right away. It's two o'clock now. The two-thirty express will get you to Manchester so that you can reach Tillman about seven-thirty. It doesn't pay to waste

any time when you're trying to get ahead of Jim
Weeks. He moves quick. Have you got
money enough?"

McNally nodded.

Thompson had come to the surface again.
He was breathing thickly, and his high, bald
forehead was damp with perspiration. "That's
bribery," he said, "and it's — dangerous."

"I'm afraid that can't be helped, Mr. Thompson," said Porter. "It's neck or nothing.
We've got to have that Tillman City stock."

There were but four people in the room when
he began speaking. There were five when he
finished, for Harvey West had grown tired of
waiting. He bowed politely.

"Good afternoon, gentlemen. Ah! Mr. Porter. How do you do? I beg your pardon for
intruding."

Porter recovered first. "No intrusion, Mr.
West. We had just finished our business."

McNally took the cue quickly.

"Mr. West?" he said interrogatively.

Harvey bowed.

"I will be at your service in a moment.
Excuse me."

Wing and Thompson had already taken the

hint, and were moving toward the door. Porter hung back, conversing in low tones with McNally. Then he bowed to West and followed the others. McNally gathered up the papers on the table, folded them, and put them in his pocket.

"Please sit down, Mr. West. What can I do for you? Wait a moment, though. Won't you smoke?" He held out his cigar case to Harvey, who took one gladly. Lighting it would give him a moment more to think, and thinking was necessary, for he didn't know what McNally could do for him. But McNally seemed to be doing his best to help him out.

"Don't you think it very warm here?" he said, as Harvey struck a match. "Something cool to drink would go pretty well. If you'll excuse me for a moment more I'll go down and see about getting it," and without waiting for a reply, McNally put on his silk hat and stepped out into the corridor.

"He certainly seems friendly," thought Harvey, as the footfalls diminished along the floor, and then he puzzled over what he should say when McNally came back. At last he smiled. "That's it," he said to himself, "I'll try to rent him that vacant suite in our office building."

When West had made up his mind that the party of four were not to meet in Wing's office, he had decided to see if they were in McNally's. He could not ask for Wing, of course, so he asked for McNally and trusted to the spur of the moment for a pretext for his call. Now that McNally's absence had enabled him to think of one he took a long breath of satisfaction. He had accomplished what he had set out to accomplish, and contrary to Jim Weeks's expressed expectation. There was no doubt that it was a combination of the C. & S. C. and Thompson's gang that was booming the M. & T. Moreover there was no doubt as to their next move. "But it won't work," he thought. "Jim owns about half of Tillman City, and anyway they'll never sell when our stock is jumping up the way it is."

And having settled this important matter he switched his train of thought off on another track. It reached Truesdale in a very short time, but it had nothing to do with M. & T., or with Mr. McNally. He took the note out of his pocket and read it through twice, and then

smoked over it comfortably for some time
before he began vaguely to wonder why Mr.
McNally didn't come back.   Five minutes later
he glanced at his cigar ash.   It was an inch
and a half long.   "That means twenty minutes," he said thoughtfully, and then it dawned
on him that things had happened which were
not down on the schedule.

He walked quickly to the telephone, and a
moment later Pease was talking to him.

"No," said the stenographer; "Mr. Weeks
went out to lunch about an hour ago.   He said
he wouldn't be back to the office this afternoon."

There had been no words wasted in the two
minutes' conversation between Porter and Mc-
Nally after Harvey's abrupt entrance, and as a
result of it, while the young secretary waited
and thought over the good stroke of work he
had done for Jim Weeks and of another good
stroke he might some day do for himself, Mr.
Frederick McNally took the two-thirty express
for Manchester and Tillman City.

CHAPTER III

POLITICS AND OTHER THINGS

HARVEY WEST was a young man. Perhaps had he been older, had his wisdom been salted with experience, he would not have put two and two together without realizing that the sum was four; but then, it is the difference between twenty-six and fifty that makes railroads a possibility. He walked slowly to the elevator and descended to the street. At the corner he paused and looked about, turning over in his mind the singular disappearance of Mr. Mc-Nally. "He can't do anything with Tillman's stock," thought Harvey. "They're solid for us." But Harvey in his brief business life had not fathomed the devious ways of the chronic capitalist. He knew that commercial honor was honeycombed with corrupt financiering, but to him the corrupt side was more or less vague, and never having soiled his fingers he

31

failed to realize the nearness of the mud.
Harvey had yet to learn that in dealing with a
municipality or with a legislature, the law of
success has but two prime factors, money and
speed.

He walked slowly over Madison Street and
turned into State.   Weeks was not in the office,
and anyway he wished to clear his mind, if
possible, before he talked with him; meanwhile
sauntering up the east side of State Street with
an eye for the shopping throng.   People interested Harvey.   He was fond of noting types,
and of watching the sandwich-men, beggars,
and shoe-string venders.   Often at noon he
would walk from Randolph Street to Harrison,
observing the shifting character of Chicago's
great thoroughfare.   To Harvey it seemed like
a river, starting clear but gradually roiled by
the smaller streams that poured in, each a
little muddier than the one next north, until it
was clogged and stagnant with the scum of the
city.   But to-day he was going north.   The
sidewalk was crowded with eager girls and
jaded women, keen on the scent of bargains.
These amused Harvey, and he smiled as he
crossed Washington Street.   A moment later

the smile brightened.   Miss Porter stood on the corner.

" Surprised to see me ? " she laughed. " Father came up unexpectedly on business, and I tagged along to do some shopping. Are you in a hurry? I suppose so. You men never lose a chance to awe us with the value of your time."

" No," Harvey replied, " I'm not at all in a hurry."

" Good, then you can help me.   I am buying a gown."

They went into Field's, and for nearly an hour Harvey " helped."   It did not take him long to realize that nowhere is a strong man more help- less than in a department store. He went through yards of samples, fingered dozens of fabrics; he discussed and suggested, all with a critical air that amused Miss Porter. She tried at first to take him seriously, but finally gave up, leaned against the counter and laughed.

" Suppose we go up to the waiting room," she said.   " You can talk, anyway."

With a smile Harvey assented, and they seated themselves near the railing, where they could look down on the human kaleidoscope below.

" By the way," said Harvey, after they had

D

chatted for some time, "this morning's *Tribune*
has a good joke on one of your Truesdale neigh-
bors. Did you see it?"

"No. Tell me about it."

"Why, it seems that he — it was Judge Black
— is up at Waupaca. He went there in a hurry
from Lake Geneva to get away from some cases
that were following him and spoiling the vacation he's been trying to get since July. He
moved so quickly that his trunk left him and
went up to Minnesota or somewhere. Well,
the Judge was asked to speak at an entertain-
ment the first night at the hotel. An hour or
so before the time set for the speech he fell into
the lake and ruined his only suit of clothes.
There wasn't a man there anywhere near his
size, so he appeared before the guests of the
Grand View Hotel in the 'bus man's overalls."

Katherine laughed heartily.

"Father will enjoy that," she said. "He
loves to laugh at Judge Black." And she
added, "I wonder where father is."

"Do you return to Truesdale to-day?" Harvey asked.

"No. Not until day after to-morrow. We
go to the South Side to dinner, father and I.

Father told me to meet him here at half-past three."

Harvey drew out his watch.

"It is after four now."

"Yes, I'm a little worried. Father is usually very prompt. He had to see some men about the railroad, but he said it wouldn't take him long. I'm afraid something has happened."

So was Harvey. The mention of Mr. Porter brought back to him certain peculiar facts, and for a moment he thought fast. Evidently something was happening. In case there was a chance of Tillman City wavering, Jim Weeks should know of Porter's activity and at once. Harvey rose abruptly.

"Excuse me. I find I have forgotten some work at the office."

"Must you go? I am sorry." She rose and extended her hand. "I shan't be at home either night or I'd ask you to come and see me. But you are coming down to Truesdale soon, remember."

"Yes," said Harvey. "Good-by."

He walked rapidly to the Washington Building. Jim had left no word, and Harvey called up the Ashland Avenue residence, but could learn nothing. The Northern Station master returned a similar report: Mr. Weeks had not been seen. Harvey sat down and rested his elbows on the desk. Already it might be too late. He called to mind Jim's business arrangements, in the hope of striking a clew by chance. He was interrupted by a few callers, whom he disposed of with a rush; and he was closing his desk with a vague idea of hunting Jim in person when he was called to the 'phone. It was the station master.

"I was mistaken, Mr. West," he said. "Fourteen has just got in from Manchester, and he says he took Mr. Weeks out at noon."

Harvey rang off and called up the M. & T. terminal station at Manchester.

"Hello. This is Chicago. Is Mr. Weeks there?"

"Well — say, hello! Hold on, central! — Will you call him to the 'phone, please?"

"Why not?"

"Where? At the shops?"

"Sorry, but I guess you'll have to interrupt him. Important business."

"Can't help it if the whole road's blocked. Get him as quick as you can and call us up. Good-by."

Harvey waited ten minutes, twenty, thirty, thirty-five — then the bell rang.

"Hello!"

"Yes."

"Not there?"

"Wait a minute. You say he took the 4.30?"

"All right. Good-by."

Harvey turned back to his desk with a scowl. He passed the next hour clearing up what was left of the day's work; then he went out to dinner, and at 6.45 met Jim Weeks at the Northern Station.

"Hello," said the magnate, "what's up?"

"Porter is," replied Harvey. "I cornered him and McNally with Thompson and Wing, and I think McNally's gone after the Tillman stock."

"I guess not," Jim smiled indulgently. "They can't touch it. Tell me what you know."

Harvey related his experience, and as one detail followed another Jim's eyebrows came together. He took out his watch and looked at it, then his eye swept the broad row of trains in the gloomy, barnlike station. The hands on the three-sided clock pointed to seven, and the Northern Vestibule Limited began to roll out on

its run to Manchester and the West.   Suddenly
Jim broke in : —

"I'm going to Tillman.   Back to-morrow."

He ran down the platform and swung himself, puffing, upon the rear steps of the re-
ceding train.   Harvey stared a moment, then
slowly walked out to the elevated.   He had not
yet learned to follow the rapid working of Jim
Weeks's mind.

In the meantime Mr. Porter was nervous.
Being unsuccessful in his search for Weeks,
and seeing the possibility of failure before him,
he greeted the hour of five with a frown ; but
he realized that there was nothing to be done.
McNally was on the field and must fight it
out alone.   It was a quarter after five when
he stepped from the elevator at Field's,
and confronted a very reproachful young
woman.

"Sorry, dear, but I couldn't get away any
sooner."

"What was it, dad ?   That old railroad ? "

" You wouldn't understand it if I told you."

Katherine frowned prettily.

"That's what you always say.   Tell me
about it."

"Well, it was very important that I should see a man before he saw another one."

"Did you see him?"

"No, I couldn't find him."

"Does it mean a loss to you, dad?"

"I hope not, dear. But we must get started."

"I thought you never would come. It was lucky that I had company part of the time."

"That's good. Who was it?"

"Mr. West."

"Mr. West?— Not Weeks's man — not—"

Katherine nodded. Her father looked at her puzzled; then his brow slightly relaxed, and he smiled. "By Jove!" he said softly. Katherine was watching him in some surprise.

"Katherine, you are a brick. You shall have the new cart. Yes, sir. I'll order it to-morrow."

"What have I done?"

"You've saved the day, my dear." Suddenly he frowned again. "Hold on; when did you see him?"

"I met him about three. I guess he was here an hour or more."

"Couldn't be better! But he must be an awful fool."

Katherine bit her lip.

"Why?" she asked quietly.

"Don't you see? If he had seen Weeks early enough they might have upset me. He must be an awful fool."

Katherine followed him to the elevator with a peculiar expression. She wondered why her father's remark annoyed her.

Before leaving Manchester Mr. McNally wired to the Tillman City Finance Committee an invitation to dine at the Hotel Tremain at 7.45 P.M. During the journey he matured his plan of campaign.

This was not likely to be more than mildly exciting, for twenty years of political and financial juggling had fitted Mr. McNally for delicate work. In his connection with various corporations he had learned the art of subduing insubordinate legislatures without friction, if not without expense, and naturally the present task offered few difficulties. That was why, after an hour or so of thought, he straightened up in his seat, bought a paper, and read it with interest, from the foreign news to the foot-ball prospects. Mr. McNally's tastes were cosmopolitan, and now that his method was deter-

mined he dismissed M. & T. stock from his
mind. He knew Tillman City, and more to the
point, he knew Michael Blaney, Chairman of
the Council Finance Committee. Finesse would
not be needed, subtlety would be lost, with
Blaney, and so Mr. McNally was prepared to
talk bluntly. And on occasion Mr. McNally
could be terseness itself.

On his arrival he took a cab for the hotel.
The Committee were on hand to meet him,
and Blaney made him acquainted with the
others.

Michael Blaney was a man of the people. • He
was tall and angular, hands and face seamed
and leathery from the work of earlier days,
eyes small and keen, and a scraggy mustache,
that petered out at the ends. He had risen by
slow but sure stages from a struggling contractor with no pull, to be the absolute monarch
of six wards; and as the other seven wards
were divided between the pro- and anti-pavers,
Blaney held the municipal reins. He still
derived an income from city contracts, but his
name did not appear on the bids.

After dinner Mr. McNally led the way to his
room, and in a few words announced that he

had come for the M. & T. stock. Blaney tipped back in his chair and shook his head.

"Can't do it, Mr. McNally. It ain't for sale."

"So I heard," said McNally, quietly, "but I want it."

"You see it's like this. When they were building the line, we took the stock on a special act—"

"I understand all that," McNally interrupted. "That can be fixed."

Williams, one of the other two, leaned over the table.

"We ain't fools enough to go up against Jim Weeks," he said.

"Don't worry about Weeks," replied McNally, "I can take care of him."

"Who are you buying for?" asked Blaney.

McNally looked thoughtfully at the three men, then said quietly:—

"I am buying for C. & S. C. Jim Weeks is all right, but he can't hold out against us."

"Well, I tell you, Mr. McNally, we can't sell."

"Why not?"

"Outside of the original terms—and they sew us up—we never could get it through the Council."

McNally folded his hands on the table and
looked at Blaney with twinkling eyes.

"That's all rot, Blaney."

"No, it ain't. The boys are right with Weeks."

"See here, Blaney. You just stop and ask
yourself what Weeks has done for you. He's
sunk a lot of your money and a lot of St.
Johns's money, to say nothing of Chicago, in
a road that never has paid and never will pay.
Why, man, the stock would be at forty now if
we hadn't pushed it up. I tell you Jim Weeks
is licked. The only way for you to get your
money back is to vote in men who can make it
go. We've got the money, and we've got the
men. It will be a good thing for Tillman City,
and a good thing" — he paused, and looked
meaningly at the three faces before him — "a
mighty good thing for you boys."

"We couldn't put it through in time for the
election anyhow."

"The eighth? That's two weeks."

"I know it, but we'd have to work the opposition."

"Talk business, Blaney. I'll make it worth
your while."

"What'll you give?"

" For the stock ? "

" Well — yes, for the stock."

" I'll give you par."

" Um — when ? "

" That depends on you. However, if you really want time, you can have it. I suppose you boys vote the stock ? "

All three nodded.

" Well, you vote for our men, and I'll sign an agreement to pay cash at par after the meeting."

" Why not now ? "

" I wouldn't have any hold on you. Anyhow, I won't pay till I get the stock, and you seem to want time."

Blaney glanced at the other two. They were watching McNally closely, and Williams was fumbling his watch chain. Blaney's eyes met McNally's.

" What'll you do for us ? " he asked. " It'll take careful work."

For answer McNally rose and went to the bed, where his bag lay open. He rummaged a moment, then returned with a pack of cards.

" Forgot my chips," he said, seating himself. " Close up, boys."

He dealt the cards with deft hands. Blaney

started to take his up, then paused with his hand over them.

"What's the ante?" he asked.

"Oh, five hundred?" McNally replied.

Blaney pushed the cards back.

"No," he said, "not enough."

Williams seconded his chief with a shake of the head.

"Well, name it yourself."

"A thousand."

McNally pursed his lips, then drew out a wallet, and counted out three thousand dollars in large bills, which he laid in the centre of the table.

"There's four playing," suggested Blaney.

McNally scowled.

"Don't be a hog, Blaney." He took up his hand, then laid it down and rose, adding, —

"Can't do anything with that hand."

The three Committeemen dropped their cards and each pocketed a third of the money. Mr. McNally fished a pad from his grip and wrote the contract binding himself to pay for the stock after the election on condition that it should be voted at his dictation. He signed it, and tossed it across the table.

"All right, Mr. McNally," said Blaney, holding out his hand.   "I guess we can see you through.   Good night."

"Good night, Blaney ; good night, boys." McNally shook hands cordially with each. "We'll have a good road here yet."

When their footfalls died away in the hall, Mr. McNally turned to the table, gathered the cards, and replaced them in his bag.   The room was close with cigar smoke, and he threw open the windows.   With the sensation of removing something offensive, he washed his hands.   He stood for a few moments looking out the window at the quiet city, then he sauntered downstairs and into the deserted parlor, seating himself at the piano.   His plump hands wandered over the keys with surprisingly delicate touch. For a short time he improvised.   Then as the night quiet stole into his thoughts, he drifted into Rubinstein's Melody in F, playing it dreamily.

CHAPTER IV

JIM WEEKS CLOSES IN

IT was midnight when Jim Weeks reached Tillman City. The next morning at breakfast he recognized Mr. McNally, and though he nodded pleasantly, his thoughts were not the most amicable. He knew that McNally meant mischief, and he also knew that McNally's mischief could be accomplished only through one man, Michael Blaney. Heretofore Blaney had not troubled Jim. Jim's power and his hold on Tillman City affairs had combined to inspire the lesser dictator with awe, and in order to obtain concessions it had been necessary only to ask for them. Jim never dealt direct with Blaney. The councilman to whom he intrusted his measures was Bridge, leader of the pro-pavers. Jim had won him by generosity in transportation of paving supplies. But when Jim left the hotel that morning he wasted no time on minority leaders. Bridge was useful to

47

prepare and introduce ordinances, but was not
of the caliber for big deals, so Jim ordered a
carriage and drove direct to Blaney's house.
Although the hour was early, the politician was
not at home. His wife, a frail little woman,
came to the door and extended a flexible speaking trumpet that hung about her shoulders.

"No," she said in reply to Jim's question,
"he's down on the artesian road watching a
job. He won't be back till noon."

The road in question leads from the city to
the artesian well a few miles away. Jim turned
his horses and went back through the town and
out toward the country. He found Blaney just
inside the city limits, sitting on a curb and over-
seeing two bosses and a gang of laborers, who
were tearing up the macadam with the destruc-
tive enthusiasm of the hired sewer digger.

"How are you, Blaney?" called Jim, pulling
up.

Blaney nodded sourly. He was a man of
bullying rather than of tactful propensities and
he could not conceal his distaste for an interview with Jim Weeks at this particular moment.
To tell the truth, he had begun to fear the
results of the agreement with McNally which

rested in his coat pocket. Weeks was a hard man to fight, and wasted no words on disloyalty. However, Blaney knew that dissimulation would profit him nothing, for to keep the changed vote a secret would be impossible; so he squared himself for a row. Jim tied his horses to a sapling and sat beside him, remarking, —

"I want to have a talk with you."

"Haven't got much time," replied Blaney, making a show of looking at his watch.

Jim smiled meaningly.

"You've got all the time I need. I want to know what you're up to with our stock."

Blaney gazed at the laborers.

"Here!" he called to a lazy Irishman, "get back there where you belong!"

"Come now, Blaney, talk business."

"What do you want to know about that stock?"

"How are you going to vote it?"

"I guess I can vote it."

"Are you going to stick to me?"

"I don't know whether I am or not. I'll do what the Council directs."

Jim gave him a contemptuous glance.

"Don't be a fool, Blaney."

E

"See here," said Blaney, rising; "what are *you* trying to do?"

Jim rose too.

"You've answered my question," he replied. "You think you can throw me out."

"I ain't throwing anybody out," muttered Blaney. He walked away and stood looking at the trench in the street which the men had sunk shoulder deep. Jim followed.

"I'm not through yet, Blaney."

"I haven't got time to talk with you," blustered the contractor. Jim stood a moment looking him over. Blaney's eyes were fixed on the Irishman.

"How much did he give you?" asked Jim, quietly.

Blaney whirled around.

"Look out," he said. "I don't know what you're talking about, but a man can't say that to me." His fists were clenched. Jim spoke without emotion.

"Drop it," he said. "I'm not here for my health. I knew all that some hours ago. If I couldn't work it any better than you've done, I'd quit. Now what I want you to do, Blaney —"

"See here, you've said enough!" Blaney was excited. "You can't come around here and bulldoze me. We've bought that stock and we'll vote it as we like, damn it; and you can go to hell!"

Jim looked at him thoughtfully, then he went to his buggy and drove back to the hotel. He saw that Blaney was frightened, but he evidently was too thoroughly bought up to be easily shaken. With what some men called his "gameness" Jim dropped Blaney from his mind for the moment, and began to plan for a desperate counter move. Before he reached the hotel the move was decided upon, and Jim was placid.

The next man to see was Bridge. Jim paused at the hotel long enough to send a message to the station agent to have a special ready in fifteen minutes; then he went to the office of his lieutenant.

Bridge was an architect with a yearning for politics. For several years he had tried to keep both irons in the fire, and as a result was not over-successful in either. But he was a shrewd, silent man, and could be trusted. Jim found him designing a stable.

"Sit down, Mr. Weeks. What brings you to Tillman?"

"Bad business," responded Jim, shortly. "Blaney's sold out to the C. & S. C."

Mr. Bridge sat upon his table and said nothing. When taken by surprise Mr. Bridge usually said nothing; that is why he had risen to the leadership of a faction.

"I don't know just what's happened," Jim went on, "but there's trouble ahead."

"Does Blaney say he's going to vote against you?"

"No," said Jim, "but he gave himself away."

"Can you block him?"

Jim passed over the question.

"I wish you'd watch him, Bridge. There's a deal on, and Frederick McNally is the other party. He's for C. & S. C. of course. Do you know him?"

Bridge shook his head.

"Well, never mind. I'll watch him. But you worry Blaney. He's a little rattled now, — I reckon McNally's soaked him, — and if you're careful you ought to find out something. I want to know just how they've fixed it."

Bridge nodded.

"I'll keep an eye on him."

"Well,"—Jim rose,—"I've got a train to catch. Good-by."

He drove rapidly to the station; the agent hurried toward him as he pulled up at the platform.

"I only got your message this minute, Mr. Weeks," he said; "there isn't a car in the yards."

"What's that?" Jim looked at his watch. "Got an engine?"

"Only the switch engine."

"I'll take that."

The agent hesitated.

"You wouldn't get through before next week," he said. "There's a couple of passenger engines in the roundhouse, but they ain't fired."

The telegraph operator leaned out of the window and broke into the conversation.

"Murphy's firing the big eleven for sixteen from Truesdale. You might take that."

"Got a good man to run it?" asked Jim.

"Jawn Donohue's on the switch engine," replied the operator. "He knows the road."

Jim dimly remembered the name Donohue. Somewhat more than a year before his manager had reduced a man of that name for crippling an engine on a flying switch.

"He's the best man you could get, Mr. Weeks," said the agent, and turning, he ran down the platform toward the freight house. Jim called after him : —

"He's got to connect at Manchester with the twelve o'clock for Chicago."

Jawn's dumpy little engine was blowing off on a siding. Jawn was oiling. He was a short man, filling out his wide overalls with an in-'em-to-stay appearance. His beard was brushy, his eyes were lost in a gray tangle of brows and lashes, and he chewed the stem of a cob pipe.

"Jawn," said the agent, excitedly, "get eleven up to the platform quick !"

Jawn turned around, lowered the oil-can, and looked at the nervous agent with impassive eyes.

"Why ?" he said slowly.

"You've got to connect with Manchester at twelve o'clock."

Jawn replaced his pipe.

"Wait till I kick them empties in on the house track. Who's it for ?"

"Don't stop for that! It's the President!"

Jawn grunted, and walked deliberately across the tracks and into the roundhouse, followed by his fireman. Murphy, the hostler, was hovering about the big throbbing locomotive, putting a final polish on the oil-cups and piston-rods. Jawn, without a word, climbed into the cab, and out over the tender, where he lifted the tank lid and peered down at the water.

"Never mind that," the agent called. "You can water up at Byron."

Jawn slowly clambered over the coal and leaned against the doorway, packing the tobacco firmly into his pipe with his fire-proof little finger.

"Young man," he said gruffly, "I run this engine for four years without taking water between here and Manchester, and I reckon I can do it agin." Then he pulled her slowly out of the roundhouse.

In the meantime, the operator had sent this message to the train despatcher at Manchester : —

Want right of way over everything. Pres. coming on light engine.

To which the despatcher replied : —

Run to Manchester extra regardless of all trains.

When the engine finally rolled into the station Jim was pacing up and down ; he was as nearly impatient as Jim Weeks could be.

"You'll have to move faster than that," he said shortly, swinging himself up the steps.

Jawn glanced at him without reply, then looked at his watch. It was twenty minutes after ten. He laid his hand upon the throttle and pulled. There was a gasp of steam, a whirring and slipping of the drive wheels, and the engine plunged forward. Jawn fingered the lever with a lover's caress. He knew old "eleven," every foot of her, every tube, bolt, and strap. As they cleared the yards, he threw her wider and wider open until she was lunging and lurching madly. The cinders beat a tattoo upon the cab, and Jim Weeks crowded up into the corner. The fireman, a strapping young fellow, threw in great shovels of coal with the regularity of a machine, pausing only to wipe his forehead with the back of his hand as the heat grew intense. When he opened the furnace door, Jim could see the glowing bed lift and stir with the jolt of the engine.

Old Jawn, perched upon his high seat, never shifted his eyes from the track ahead. His face wore the usual scowl, but betrayed no emotion. Perhaps his teeth gripped the pipe-stem harder than usual, but then, it was a pregnant hour for Jawn. The feel of the old pet under his hand made his heart jump, and brought the hope that a successful run might lead him back to his own. Jawn knew that he deserved something better than a switch engine in the division yards, he knew that he was the best engineer on the road, but he had steeled himself against hope. As they whirled past the mile-posts his emotion grew. He felt that the President was watching him closely, and he coaxed the steel thing into terrific speed. The cab grew hotter and hotter. Jim loosened his grip on the seat long enough to unbutton his collar and to twist his handkerchief around his neck. The fireman was dripping, but Jawn sat immovable as marble. They whirled past little stations with a sudden roar. At Brushing-ham a passenger train lay on the siding. There was a mottled flash of yellow, then they were by, and for an instant Jawn smiled. He hadn't passed Jack Martin like that for years.

Then they struck the hills.   Up with a snort, over with a groan, and down with a rumble and slide, they flew.   Here Jawn's eyes shifted to the water gauge.   Jim locked one arm around the window post, and sat with eyes fixed on his watch.   The minute hand crept around to eleven, passed it, and on to five, ten, fifteen, twenty, twenty-five.   At thirty-five clusters of cottages began to shoot by.   Jawn's arm began to straighten — the roar diminished a trifle. Thirty-seven they passed rows of coal-laden flat cars ; thirty-nine, they slackened through a tangle of tracks; forty-one, the big engine rolled under the train shed and stopped in a cloud of steam.

Jim stepped down and stretched himself. The fireman had staggered back into the tender, and lay in a heap, fanning himself with his cap.   Jawn took a final glance at the water gauge, then he swung around and removed his cold pipe.

"Mr. Weeks," he said gruffly, "I brung ye a hundred and three mile in eighty-one minutes. There ain't another man on the line could 'a' done it.   I reckon that's why there's nothing for me but a switch engine."   Without waiting for a reply he seized an oil-can and swung out of the cab. Jim followed in silence, and hurried away with a grim smile.

At two-thirty Jim was in his Chicago office. For some time he was closeted with Myers, treasurer of the road, then he closed his desk and went out. He spent an hour with Spencer, a capitalist and an M. & T. director. From four to six he was locked in his office, going through his various collateral securities. At six he locked his office and went home with a feeling of relief. The battle was on, and Jim was ready. There would be a meeting at his house that evening between Spencer, Myers, and himself; not a long meeting, but one productive of results.

CHAPTER V

HARVEY WEST liked to be comfortable. His rooms were in a quiet apartment house on the West Side, within easy reach of the Metropolitan Elevated, and not far from the big house where Jim Weeks held bachelor sway. Harvey was not a musician, but a good piano stood in his sitting room. He had accumulated a few etchings and two bronzes; and on the centre table were piled the latest books. Harvey read these about as he listened to Grand Opera — he recognized that a man should keep in touch with such things. In a vague way he enjoyed them, but he was too honest to cultivate the glib generalities that give so many men a rating as connoisseurs of art, music, and literature. Harvey liked action. Business appealed to him, anything with motion and excitement; then, after the fever of the day, he was drawn to a few friends and a good cigar. But back behind

60

his straightforward democratic temperament
there was a dash of good blood, the sifting down
of generations of gentlemen and gentlewomen,
that accounted for Harvey's inherent good
taste. He could not criticise the technique of a
picture, but he never selected a poor one. And
the few books he really liked were the kind one
can read once a year with profit.

Early on this Tuesday evening Harvey was
trying to read, but his eyes would wander and
his brow contract. At intervals he would turn
in his chair and endeavor to bring his thoughts
back to the book. Finally he shut it with a
bang and, walking to the window, stood looking
out over the city. It had been a hard day for
Harvey. He had passed hours waiting to learn
the result of Jim's efforts to head off McNally.
The news that C. & S. C. would undoubtedly
control the Tillman City stock at election had
been closely followed by the discovery of unexpected strength in the opposition directors.
People used to say of Jim that he was never so
happy as when fighting in his last ditch, but
Harvey derived no pleasure from such operations. On this occasion he was particularly
troubled. He felt that his failure to tend to

business the preceding afternoon had contributed largely to the loss of Tillman City; and, worst of all, what a fool Miss Porter must think him.

The boulevard below was hedged with two long rows of gas-lamps which converged far away to the south. Sounds of the street floated up to him — the clatter of hoofs on the asphalt, disjointed conversations from wheelmen, juvenile calls and whistles. Harvey looked down at the strolling crowds on the sidewalk, and felt lonely. He turned away from the window, and took a cigar from the hospitable box on the mantel. Near the box was a kodak picture of Miss Porter which he had taken some time before. He held the picture to the light, and gazed at it earnestly. "You had a fine laugh over me yesterday, didn't you, when your father told you all about it?"

Harvey's big sitting room was popular. His friends had the comfortable habit of dropping in at almost any hour of the day or night, sure of a hearty welcome. But to-night the thought of visitors caused him to replace the picture suddenly, seize his hat and stick, and start out for — somewhere. At first he entertained a dim notion of going to Lincoln Park, so he took the elevated down town, and started north on the Clark Street cable. But as the car jolted along, he remembered that the band did not play Tuesday evenings. He might take in the electric fountain, but in the crowd you couldn't go about and look at people without being in other people's way. Harvey was fond of the great public, but he liked to hold himself in the background. He rode past the Park under the long row of elms, gazing absently at the thronging walk where the middle strata of North Side humanity take their evening promenade. Passing the Park, he decided to go on to the Bismarck, where he could be among people and yet remain alone.

A few minutes before eight he walked between the brown dragons which guard the entrance, and crossed the raised pavilion between the street and the garden. At the head of the stairs he paused a moment, then he turned aside and seated himself at a table near by, where he could lean against the railing and overlook the crowd below.

It was still somewhat early, and the long rows of white tables stood vacant. By daylight

the trees in a summer garden wear a home-
sick look, but to-night the festooned incandes-
cent lamps spread a soft yellow light through
the foliage, already thinned, though the night
was warm, by the touch of September; while
high up on their white poles the big arcs threw
down a weird blue glare, casting a confusion of
half-opaque shadows upon the gravelled earth.
Far to the front was the stage with its half
dome; the double-bass was tuning his instrument, a few others were sorting music or running over difficult passages.

By this time the crowd was pouring in and
spreading among the tables. Harvey leaned
back and watched the almost unbroken line
that moved from the gate to the steps. There
were a great many family groups, with here
and there a chaperoned party from the suburbs.
A sound of scraping and squealing and grunt-
ing from the stage announced the orchestral
preliminaries. There was a scattering fusillade
of applause as the tall conductor appeared.
Looking through the trees, Harvey could see
him rap his stand and raise both arms. The
concert was on. Harvey's glance shifted back
to the stairway, and he started. On the bottom

step, looking about for a vacant table, was William C. Porter. Behind him, standing, with head thrown back, was Miss Katherine Porter. For a moment she looked at the shifting scene before her. Harvey noted with hungry eyes the poise of her figure. Then she turned deliberately, and bowed to Harvey with a bright smile.

A little later, as Harvey sat alone listening to the music, Mr. Porter appeared, picking his way toward the centre aisle. Harvey watched him idly. He finally reached the stairway, and came straight to Harvey's table.

"Good evening, Mr. West," he said, holding out his hand. "Won't you join us? We shall be here for an hour, anyway."

Harvey rose, and looked across the diagonal line of tables. Miss Porter was leaning forward with a smile. Harvey's mind had been made up, but he changed it and followed Mr. Porter.

Katherine received him brightly and immediately put him at ease. For the time he forgot that Mr. Porter and he were nominal enemies. Mr. Porter talked entertainingly of the people about them, a subject which Harvey could continue with intelligence; and he was gratified to

F

note the interest in the daughter's eyes as he commented on the oddities of human character.

They were looking at a party of Germans, who sat listening to the music with the stolid interest of the race, when Mr. Porter rose and beckoned.   Katherine nodded to some one behind Harvey.   A moment later he was shaking hands with Mr. McNally.

"We've been watching for you for some time," said Mr. Porter, as McNally took the vacant chair.

"Have you?" McNally smiled easily. "I wish you had said that, Miss Porter."

"Oh, Mr. McNally, you know I was hoping for you."

Harvey's eyes betrayed him, for she added in a bantering tone, —

"We must say such things to Mr. McNally, Mr. West; if we don't, he gets simply unbearable."

McNally looked at her with an amused expression. Evidently they understood each other. As the banter continued, Harvey began to feel uncomfortable. He tried to listen to the orchestra, which was playing a lively march.

"Good, isn't it?" said Miss Porter to Harvey.

" Splendid," he replied.

" Do you think so?" observed Mr. McNally. "Seems to me Bunge's a little off to-night. Too much drum. Queer motions, hasn't he?"

Herr Bunge's motions were queer. He was very tall and spare, with an angular, smooth-shaven face, and with a luxuriant growth of hair that waved and flopped in the gentle breeze. His long arms were principally elbow, and they swayed and crooked and jerked as though he were pulling the music down out of the air. At times when he turned to the be-lated second violins, his gaunt profile would appear in silhouette against a glare of electric light.

" Do you know," said McNally, fingering his programme, " Bunge ought to stick to this kind of stuff. Last week I heard him play some of the Queen Mab music, and it was wilful slaugh-ter. Poor old Berlioz would have sobbed aloud if he had heard it."

Harvey felt awkward. He could not follow McNally's comments, and it humiliated him. Miss Porter was quick to observe his silence, and endeavored to draw him into the conversation, while Mr. McNally seemed determined to hold the reins. There was some good-natured fencing, then Mr. Porter rose.

"You'll excuse us, Mr. West," he said pleasantly. "We have an engagement for the latter part of the evening."

"Yes," added his daughter, "we promised to go out to Edgewater — the Saddle and Cycle, you know."

Harvey bowed and stood immovable, as father, daughter, and Mr. McNally left the garden. She had given him a quick glance, and he wondered what it meant. He sat down and absently broke the straws in his glass. The orchestra had stopped, and a buzz of conversation floated into the foliage. White-clad waiters bustled about with trays piled high.

After another number he started for home, blue and angry. As he left the elevated and walked down Ashland Avenue, he saw that Jim's house was lighted up, and he crossed over. Jim and he were better friends than their relative positions indicated. Neither had family ties, and Jim's interest in the younger man was perhaps the nearest approach to sentiment he had felt for years. He seldom openly showed his regard, but Harvey was perfectly conscious of it, and he valued it highly.

Jim was sitting alone at the table in the library. He greeted Harvey by tipping back and waving toward a seat. The table was littered with papers.

"How are you?" said Jim. "We've stolen a march on you."

Harvey smiled, and threw himself wearily into a chair at the other end of the table.

"What is it?" he asked. "C. & S. C. again?"

Jim nodded, and drawing out his cigar case, he took one and tossed the case down to Harvey, then said : —

"Yes, and I think we've got 'em down. We've issued some more stock." He leaned on the table and spoke in a confidential tone. "And I reckon Porter'll be doing a hornpipe when he finds it out."

"Who took it?" asked Harvey.

"Spencer, Myers, and I. The books haven't been closed, you know."

Harvey blew out a thin cloud of smoke, and looked at it meditatively.

"Nine thousand shares," continued Jim. "If

there's anything he can do now, he's welcome to try."

"Do you think he will try?"

"Oh, yes, he'll come at us with something or other. But he can't do a thing."

There was a long silence, then Harvey said,—

"You didn't pay cash for the stock?"

"Ten per cent," Jim replied.

Harvey fingered his cigar. Every new move of Jim's bewildered him. Jim's imperturbability, and his eagerness for a fight where some men would be discouraged, were qualities that Harvey was slow in acquiring. His admiration for Jim amounted almost to reverence. Perhaps had he realized the bitter fighting that was yet to come, if he could have foreseen the part that he was to play with zeal and judgment, he would have been even more bewildered, but Harvey was plucky enough; it needed only the right circumstances to develop him.

"If he does fight," said Jim, breaking the silence, "if he succeeds in landing on us, why, then, look out for war. I'll put my last cent into M. & T. before I'll give him a chance at it."

"Is he likely to grab the road?"

"Maybe he'll try. But I'll have five hundred men with guns in his way. I'll tell you, West, I'm not going to give in. I never have yet."

"No," said Harvey, thoughtfully, "I don't believe you have." And he added, "I saw Porter to-night."

"Where?"

"·Up at the Bismarck. McNally was with him."

"Anybody else?"

"His daughter."

"Pretty girl, I hear."

"Yes," — Harvey spoke slowly, — "she is. A very pretty girl. Her father seems to be a gentleman."

"Oh, Porter's all right. He's doing what 'most any man in his place would do. It's business. There's nothing personal in it."

"I suppose not," Harvey replied. "It's still a little odd to me. I'm afraid I'd want to break his head."

Jim laughed.

"You'll get over that. I reckon you haven't got anything against his daughter."

"Perhaps not," said Harvey; "but that's different."

"Oh, is it?"

Harvey sat for a moment without reply, then he tossed his half-smoked cigar into the ash-tray and rose.

"Don't go, West. I shall be up for a long while."

"I'm tired," Harvey replied. "I need sleep. Good night."

Harvey walked home slowly. Once in his room, he did not light up; instead he drew an easy-chair to the window and stretched out where he could feel the breeze. It had been a strange evening. He went back over the conversation in the Bismarck. Katherine had seemed even prettier than usual; but before every picture of her rose the calm, smiling face of McNally — McNally with his pudgy hands and his cool blue eyes, his ease and his well-placed comment. Harvey rested an elbow on the sill and looked out the window. The crowds were gone now. No sound came save the rustle of the leaves and the occasional rumble of the elevated trains. The moon was clouded, but over the trees the stars were out, as clear and soft as on other evenings that had not seemed so dreary. He turned away and walked over to the mantel, where Katherine's picture leaned against the wall. He found it without striking a light, and brought it to the window. By the dim light from the street and the sky, he could see her face in faint outline.

"Well, Miss Katherine," he said, looking into the shadowy eyes, "I guess Jim Weeks isn't the only fighter here."

CHAPTER VI

JUDGE BLACK

THERE are two kinds of business men: those who make their business at once work and play, a means of acquiring wealth and a most exciting game whose charms make all other games seem flat and unprofitable; and another class who, though they may enjoy work, turn for recreation to whist or philanthropy or golf. Porter belonged to the latter class. He went into the fight against Jim Weeks simply because he hoped it would make him richer, and it did not occur to him that he could enjoy the action. On Wednesday morning he sat in his office wondering if he could not get away to the Truesdale golf links for a match that afternoon.

He looked over the ground carefully, and could see no way by which Weeks could save himself from defeat, for the control of Tillman City gave C. & S. C. a majority of the stock. Weeks's allies were deserting him, so that he now had a bare majority in the Board of Directors. Anyway, McNally would be on the ground in case Jim should try to do anything.

"Well," thought Porter, "I'll go. I guess it's safe enough." He had closed his desk when the door opened and an office boy came in with a telegram. Porter tore it open listlessly, but his indolence vanished as he read the first line. The message was from Manchester, and it read as follows : —

M. & T. subscription book stubs show issue of nine thousand shares new stock to Weeks, Myers, and Spencer, ten per cent paid, dated yesterday.

POWERS.

When a man finds himself in an ambush, or when an utterly unexpected attack is made upon him, he shows what he is. It was characteristic of Porter that after the moment of dazed unrealization had passed he began almost mechanically to plan a break for cover; he wished that he had not gone into the fight, and berated his stupidity in not foreseeing the move; it had not occurred to him that the subscription for the stock had not closed long ago. After a few minutes of vain search for an avenue of retreat, he saw that it was too late to do anything but fight it out; Jim Weeks was not likely to let an antagonist off easily.

He called to his secretary: "Telephone Shields to come over here, will you, as soon as he can? And ask McNally to come too." While he was waiting for them he sat quite still in his big chair and thought hard, but he could see no way of countering the blow.

The two men he had sent for came into the office together. Porter did not rise. With a nod of greeting he handed the yellow envelope to McNally, who whistled softly as he caught its import, and passed it on to Shields, an attorney for the C. & S. C., an emotionless, noncommittal man.

"Hm — it looks as though that beat you," he said slowly.

Porter lost his nerve and his temper too for a moment. He rose quickly and took a step toward the lawyer.

"Hell, man!" he exclaimed angrily. "We can't be beat. We've got to get out of this some way. That's what you're here for." Then he recovered himself. "I beg your pardon, Shields. Sit down, and we'll talk this business over."

For nearly an hour the three men sat in earnest consultation; then the secretary was called in.

"Find out if Judge Black is in Truesdale," said Porter. "If he is, I want to talk to him." Then he turned to Shields.

"That's our move," he said. "We can allege fraud on the ground that the stock was issued secretly and with the purpose of influencing the election. Black's the man for that business."

"It isn't much of a case, mind you," said Shields. "I'm afraid that Weeks's action is not illegal, and that a court would sustain it, but it's possible to raise a question that it will take time to decide."

"That's all we need," said Porter, with a sigh of relief. "If we raise the question, Black will do the rest."

It was several minutes before the secretary came back from the telephone.

"Well, did you get him?" asked Porter.

"No," said the secretary; "he isn't in Truesdale."

"Where is he?"

"I couldn't find out. His stenographer wouldn't tell me."

"Wouldn't tell you, eh?" said Porter. "Just get Truesdale again; I'll talk with that young man myself."

When he began talking his voice was mild and persuasive, and Shields and McNally listened expectantly. As the minutes went by and he did not get the information he wanted, it became evident that the cocksure young man at the other end of the line was rasping through what was left of Porter's patience as an emery wheel does through soft iron. As might be expected, the process was accompanied with a shower of sparks. Porter's voice rose and swelled in volume until at last he shouted, "You don't care who I am? Why, you damned little fool —" and then he stopped, for a sharp click told him that he was cut off, even from the central office, and he was not angry enough to go on swearing at an unresponsive telephone.

For a moment he stood biting his lip in a nervous effort to control himself, then he joined feebly in the laughter the other two men had raised against him. A moment later he pulled out his watch, and turning to McNally said : —

"Keep your eye on Weeks, will you? I'm going to Truesdale on the eleven-thirty to find Black. Good-by."

Katherine was not surprised when twenty minutes later her father appeared and told her his plans. That was the train she had expected they would take.

"I'm going along too," she said. "You're going to play golf this afternoon, aren't you?"

"No," replied her father, shortly, "I'm not going to play golf. I'm going to play something else."

The five-hour ride to Truesdale was for the most part a silent one. Katherine knew that her father was worried about something, and when he was worried he never liked to talk, so she asked no questions and made no attempt to draw him away from what troubled him. Only when they reached Truesdale and her father was about to help her into the cart that stood waiting she stopped long enough to kiss him and say : —

"Don't bother too much about it, dad. And don't plan any business for this evening; I

want you to take me out on the river." As she
turned the cart around and started up the broad
smooth street toward home she frowned, and
thought, "I wish he would tell me more about
things. I believe I could help."

Porter went straight to Judge Black's to continue his conversation with the stenographer,
but it needed no more than a glance to convince
him of the futility of trying to get any information from that source.

The new stenographer was a boyish-looking
person who tried to convince one that he was
much older than his appearance would indicate.
He had big feet and a high voice ; he used only
the bottom notes for conversational purposes
save when in unwary moments Nature would assert herself in a hoarse falsetto. He patronized
Mr. Porter. He said that the Judge had left
town the week before, and that he would probably be back in about ten days. He would send
him no messages whatever, from anybody : those
were Judge Black's orders.

The young man seemed willing to go on talking at great length, and he doubtless would
have done so had not Porter suddenly left the
room. The Vice-President had thought of a

possible clew. He walked rapidly to the rail-road ticket office and spoke to the agent.

"Did Judge Black leave town a few days ago?" he asked.

"Yes, sir," answered the agent. "I don't remember just what day, but he went up on twenty-two."

"Oh, he went east then. Do you remember where?"

"His ticket read to Chicago."

Porter walked away thoroughly disappointed. The chance had looked like a good one and there seemed to be no other. But he must in some way find the Judge; he could not wait for him. The first thing he did was to call up McNally by telephone and repeat to him what the agent had said. He told McNally to find out at what hotel the Judge had stayed, if at any, and to look for anything which might prove a clew to his whereabouts. "It's a wild-goose chase, I know," he concluded; "but then you may manage to turn up something." He knew that McNally would do everything that could be done in Chicago toward finding the missing Judge, so he went to work along other lines.

G

Judge Black was a member of two fishing clubs, one at Les Chenaux Islands, near Mackinac, and the other about forty miles north of Minneapolis, so Porter sent long and urgent telegrams to both these places. Then he began making long shots, working through a list of more or less likely places, which his knowledge of Black's tastes and habits enabled him to get together. Just before dinner a message came from McNally : —

Black at Sherman House Friday. Clerk says he took three-thirty train on Northwestern for Lake Geneva. Can run him down in morning.

Thursday morning the two little telegraph boys at Lake Geneva and the one at William's Bay had a busy time of it, for Porter and McNally between them kept the wires hot; but neither hide nor hair of Judge Alonzo Black could they discover. From ten o'clock on through an interminable day the messages kept coming back, 'not delivered.' At half-past four Porter telephoned his lieutenant to go to the lake and continue the search in person.

At seven Katherine and her father sat down to dinner. She had known all day that something was going wrong with her father's affairs, and she could read in his silent preoccupied manner that he had not yet been able to see a way out of the difficulty. She knew that she could not make him forget his troubles. Many vain attempts had taught her that, so she waited. The long dinner wore on Porter's nerves; once he rose suddenly and walked toward his library, but stopped short when he reached the door and came back to the table. Then he drummed on the arm of his chair.

"Two days more of this," he said, with a nervous laugh, "and that man Black will have my life to answer for."

"Judge Black?" asked Katherine. "What has he done?"

"Done? He's disappeared off the face of the earth just at this particular moment when I've got to have him here."

"Why," cried Katherine, "I know where he is. He's at the Grand View Hotel —" she paused and leaned forward, her elbows on the table and her hands clasped before her. "It's some place up in Wisconsin that sounds like alpaca. Waupaca — that's it. Grand View Hotel, Waupaca, Wisconsin."

"Are you sure that's right?" he asked.
"How do you know?"

"Mr. West told me," she answered. "There
was such a good joke on him in the paper. I
meant to tell you about it."

But Porter was smiling over something else.
After a moment he said: —

"We'd have been swamped long ago in this
M. & T. business if it hadn't been for the kind
services of that wise and valuable young man,
West. I think I'll pay him a regular salary
after this to keep him on the other side in all
the fights I get into. Lord, what a fool he is!"

He left the room so abruptly that he did not
see how Katherine's cheeks reddened, nor how
her lips pressed together in vexation. If he
had he would not have known the reason for it
any more than Katherine did.

Rainbow Lake is pretty in the daytime,
but it is beautiful under the moonlight when
you can stretch out distances and imagine that
the lights at Bagley's Landing are those of a
city twenty miles away, and when the solid pine
groves on Maple and Government islands loom
up big and black. The Judge was enjoying his

vacation the better for its lateness. He had bolted his supper early enough to secure his favorite chair in the best part of the piazza : a mandolin orchestra was playing a waltz from " The Serenade," and playing it well, the Judge thought. He threw away the match with which he had lighted his third cigar — to keep off the mosquitoes, he blandly told his conscience — and leaned back in the Morris chair, thinking how congruously comfortable it all was, now that he had his own clothes and the 'bus man could work without soiling his other suit.

A clerk came out of the office, peered about in the half light for a moment, and approached the Judge, touching him on the shoulder.

"Judge Black," he said, " Truesdale wants to talk to you on the 'phone."

Five minutes later the legal luminary came out of the telephone box. He was swearing earnestly, but softly, out of deference to the candy-and-cigar girl. He walked slowly across the office.

"There's a train for Chicago at 8.30, isn't there ? " he asked.

"Yes," said the clerk. " Do you want to take it ? "

There was another pianissimo interlude, at the end of which the clerk was given to understand that he should order the 'bus for that train. Then the Judge went back for his chair, but it was occupied by a little girl who was just too old to be asked to sit somewhere else.

As Jim Weeks had said, Thompson wouldn't fight, and Porter realized this quite as well as Jim. The recalcitrant Vice-President played no part in Porter's calculations except as a somewhat blundering and obstinate tool. But on Friday morning Thompson's office boy announced Mr. Porter. Porter stated his case clearly. It was his plan to remove Weeks and Myers by judicial order from the Board of Directors. That would leave the opposition a majority of the board. Then Thompson was to call a meeting and assume control of the books. That done, the battle would be decided, and the election a mere formality. Thompson was badly rattled, for he hadn't a grain of sand in his composition, but in the end he conquered his fears and agreed to play the part Porter assigned to him.

At half-past two a disjointed-looking train panted into the Harrison Street Station, and

Judge Black climbed disconsolately out of the smoker. There was a coating of cinders on the top of his derby hat; there were drifts of cinders in the curl of the brim; there were streaks of cinders along the lines where his coat wrinkled; and there was one cinder in his left eye which gave him so leery and bibulous an aspect that an old lady who narrowly escaped colliding with him turned and looked after him in indignation, being half minded to go back and plead with him to lead a better life.

It was fifteen minutes later when the Judge reached Porter's office, but before three o'clock he had signed an order enjoining James Weeks and Johnson Myers from acting as directors of, or from interfering in any way with, the affairs of the corporation known as the Manchester & Truesdale Railroad Company, and from voting the nine thousand shares of stock in that company which had been issued September 25th.

CHAPTER VII

BETWEEN THE LINES

On Friday afternoon Harvey closed his desk
with a feeling of relief.   There had been plenty
of work for the past few days, and Harvey's
thoughts had acquired such wandering habits
that his work seemed harder than usual.   He
had not seen Katherine since Tuesday evening,
but another note, dated Thursday evening, was
in his coat pocket.   He read it again : —

My dear Mr. West: As you have inferred from the
postmark I am back at Truesdale; we returned Wednesday. I have about despaired of seeing you here, at least
of your own free will, so I have decided to kidnap you.
Will you come to a coaching party Saturday afternoon —
or rather a brake party? We shall start from our house,
weather permitting, at four o'clock, and drive out to Oakwood, returning by moonlight. Please don't let any stupid business interfere with your coming down and having
a jolly time.

Cordially,
Katherine Porter.

Harvey slowly folded the note and replaced it in his pocket. Then he spoke to Jim.

"Mr. Weeks, will you need me to-morrow?"

Jim looked up pleasantly. Since the recent issue of M. & T. stock, Jim's eyes had smiled almost continuously.

"Guess not," he replied. "Going away?"

"Just over Sunday."

"You aren't going anywhere near Truesdale, are you?"

"Why, yes."

Jim whirled around to his desk and rummaged through some pigeonholes.

"I want to get word to a man down there," he said, — "some fellow that Fox talks about, who has a good team to sell. I thought I had his card. Well, never mind, I'll call up Fox in the morning and get his name and address. Then if you have time" — Jim smiled — "you might talk with him and see what they are. Don't commit yourself; just size things up."

Harvey bowed.

"I don't believe you need come around in the morning. I'll call you up or wire you. But don't lose any dinners on account of it."

The next morning Harvey went to Truesdale.

The Oakwood Club House stands on a knoll some eight miles up the river from Truesdale. Giant elms shade the wide veranda, while others droop over the white macadam drive that swings steeply down to the bridge and vanishes in a grove of oak, hickory, and birch. If you stand on the steps and look west, you can see, through the immediate foliage, the Malden County hills, their blue tops contrasting with the nearer green of the valley. To the left, an obtruding wing checks the view; on the right, leading straight down to the river, is a well-worn path.

After dinner the party strolled up and down the veranda, gradually separating into couples. The twilight creeping down found Harvey and Miss Porter alone by the railing. She stood erect, looking out over the valley, her scarlet golf jacket thrown back, her hair disordered by the long ride and curling about her face. Harvey watched her in silence. He was glad that she was tall; he liked to meet her eyes without looking down. He had often tried to remember the color of those eyes. Presently she turned and looked at him.

"They're gray," he said, half to himself.

"No," she replied; "sometimes they are brown and sometimes green. They are not gray."

Harvey leaned forward.

"I'm sure they are."

For a moment they stood looking into each other's eyes, then she turned away with a little laugh and removed her sailor hat, swinging it from her hand.

"Look," she said, with an impulsive gesture toward the west. Harvey followed her gaze. The dark was settling into the valley. There were splotches of foliage and waves of meadow, with a few winding strips of silver where the river broke away from the trees. "And to think that we have only a few more such days."

"Yes,"—he spoke softly,—"we don't see things like that in Chicago."

"Why don't you come to Truesdale?"

"So long as Mr. Weeks stays in Chicago, I am likely to be there too."

"You are fond of Mr. Weeks?"

"Yes, I am."

"I never met him—I've heard a great deal about him." She sat upon the railing and leaned back against a pillar, her eyes turned to the foliage. "Father says he is a good business man."

"He is."

"Mr. West," she threw her head back with a peremptory toss — "I want you to tell me something."

"Wait," he replied, "come to the river. Then I'll tell you anything."

She smiled, but acquiesced, and they went down the path. Harvey drew up a cedar boat and extended his hand, but she stepped lightly aboard without his aid. Harvey pushed away from the bank and began slowly to paddle against the current.

"Now," he said, "the Sister Confessor may proceed."

She looked up at him. He thought she was smiling, but she spoke earnestly.

"I want you to tell me about this M. & T. fight."

"I don't believe there is anything to tell."

"You think I am not interested."

"No — not that."

"You men are all alike. You think a girl can't understand business." She seemed to be musing. "You like a girl who is helpless and fluttery, who can be patronized."

"No," said Harvey, "not that either."

"I wish you would tell me."

"How much do you know?"

Before replying she looked out over the water for several moments. Harvey rested his oars and waited. She turned to him, still musing.

"I'll be frank," she said. "I am not going to say how much I know, but I want you to tell me all about it."

Harvey began to row.

"Of course," she went on, "I have heard father's friends talking."

Harvey smiled.

"You puzzle me," he remarked.

"Why should any one wish to get control of your road?"

"Because there is coal on the line."

"Is Mr. Weeks firmly in control?"

Harvey leaned over the oars.

"I wish I knew —" he hesitated. "Are we good friends?"

"I can speak for myself."

"Why are you interested in this business?"

"Because — well, I will tell you the truth. Of course I know that father and Mr. Weeks are — I suppose you would call it fighting.

Father doesn't understand how I could ask you down to-day."

" I am glad you did."

" I wanted you to feel that — you see we have been good friends, and it would be too bad to let a thing like this — don't you understand ? "

Harvey leaned forward and impulsively extended his hand.   She drew back.

" Just shake hands," said Harvey.   He clasped hers firmly, releasing it with a quiet " Thank you."

They were drifting down stream under the trees with no sound save a faint rustle from overhead.   Strands of moonlight sifted through the foliage, blurring the east bank into shadow.

" Do you know what I am thinking of ? " Harvey asked in a low tone.   She smiled faintly and shook her head.   They swung into a patch of moonlight, and for a moment their eyes met; then she looked away and said, —

" We must go back."

" It isn't late," Harvey remonstrated.

" We must go back."

Harvey obediently took up the oars, then hesitated.

" Please don't stay here," she said.

They went up the path in silence.   The brake

stood at the steps, and the other members of
the party were laughing and talking on the
veranda. Harvey stopped before they left the
shadow. Miss Porter walked a few steps, then
turned and faced him.

"What is the matter?" he asked. "Can't
you trust me? Are you afraid of me?"

She came forward and laid her hand upon
his arm.

"Don't misunderstand me," she said with
hesitation. "If I were as sure of myself as I
am of you — Come, they are watching us."

An hour later they stood at Mr. Porter's door.

"Good night," said Harvey, but she lingered.

"Shall I see you to-morrow?"

"Do you think I had better come?"

"Why not?"

"Perhaps your father —"

"I want you to. Anyway," smiling, "father
is in Chicago."

Harvey smiled too.

"I'll send the trap for you, and we'll drive —
at ten, say. I suppose you are at the hotel."

"Yes," said Harvey. "Good night."

Mr. Porter's summer home was located on
the river bank, something less than a mile from

the Truesdale Hotel. The walk was somewhat lonely, and it gave Harvey time to think. At first he was bewildered. She had seemed to be mistress of the situation, but at any rate he had told her nothing about M. & T. affairs. There came into his mind a suspicion that she knew more than she had led him to believe, for she would naturally not let a man who had no claim upon her sway her loyalty to her father. And yet, those eyes were honest. They had looked into his with an expression that would charm away graver doubts than his. "I'll make her tell me," he thought. "I'll find out to-morrow just what she means, and if — " In spite of himself, Harvey's heart beat fast at thought of the possibilities which lay behind that "if." From doubt, he drifted back into a review of the evening. He called up pictures of her on the brake, on the boat, or on the shaded path. When he reached the hotel he sat down on the veranda and lighted a cigar. "Yes," he repeated to himself, "I'll make her tell me." But in the morning, after a more or less steady sleep, Harvey looked out at the calm sunlight and changed his mind. "I'll wait," he thought, "and see what happens."

At ten, the Porter trap stood in front of the hotel, and Harvey climbed into the trap and took the reins. As he started, a telegraph boy ran down the steps calling to him. Harvey took the yellow envelope and with a thought of Jim's errand he thrust it between his teeth, for the horses were prancing. Later he stuffed it into his pocket until he should reach the Porters'. The drive was exhilarating, and by the time he pulled up in the porte-cochère he had himself well in control. She did not keep him waiting, and they were soon whirling down the old river road.

Katherine was in a bright mood. For a space they talked commonplaces. Harvey thought of the telegram, but dared not take his attention from the horses until they should run off a little spirit, so he let them go.

"Isn't it splendid," she said, drawing in the brisk air and looking at the broad stream on their right. "Do you know, I never see the river without thinking of the old days when this country was wild. It seems so odd to realize that Tonty and La Salle paddled up and down here. They may have camped where we are now. Sometimes in the evenings when we are

H

on the river, I imagine I can see a line of
canoes with strange, dark men in buckskin, and
painted Indians, and solemn old monks, with
Father Hennepin in the first canoe. So many
curious old memories hover over this stream."

The horses were slowing. Harvey said
abruptly, —

"Will you mind if I open a telegram?"

"Certainly not." She reached out and took
the reins. Harvey opened the envelope with
his thumb. He read the message twice, then
lowered it to his knees with a puzzled expression.

"Bad news?" asked Miss Porter.

"I don't know. Read it if you like."

She handed back the reins and read the
following : —

Mr. Harvey West:
     You are receiver M. & T. Come to Manchester at
once.
                                        Weeks.

"Well," he said, "what do you think?"

She slowly folded the paper and creased it
between her fingers.

"Can you make it?" she asked.

Harvey looked at his watch. "Train goes at eleven. I've got thirteen minutes."

"Turn around. It's only three miles. We can do it."

Harvey pulled up and turned. Then he hesitated.

"How about the team?" he said; "I can't take you home."

"Never mind that. Quick; you can't lose any time. I'll get the team back."

Harvey nodded and gripped the reins, and in a moment the bays were in their stride. Harvey's hands were full, and he made no effort to talk. Miss Porter alternately watched him and the horses.

"They can do better than that. You'll have to slow up in town, you know." And Harvey urged them on.

As they neared the town, Harvey spoke.

"Will you look at my watch?"

She threw back his coat and tugged at the fob until the watch appeared. "Three minutes yet. We're all right."

But a blocked electric car delayed them, and they swung up to the platform just at train-time. Harvey gripped her hand: —

"Good-by.   I shan't forget this."

But though her eyes danced, she only answered, "Please hurry!"

As Harvey dropped into a seat and looked out the car window, he saw her sitting erect, holding the nervous team with firm control. And he settled back with a glow in his heart.

CHAPTER VIII

JUDGE GREY

On Friday, after Jim Weeks had told Harvey that he was free to go to Truesdale, he followed the young man almost fondly with his eyes and he did not at once resume the work which awaited him. For Harvey's request had set him thinking. During years that passed after the day when he took his last drive with Ethel Harvey, he had not dared to think of her. Later when he heard of her death, he did not try to analyze the impulse which led him to offer a position to Harvey. As he grew to know the young fellow he gradually admitted to himself his fondness for him, and now that he believed that Harvey was in love, he allowed himself for the first time the luxury of reminiscence.

The old Louisville days came back to him when he and Ethel rode together through country lanes and he loved her. The wound was healed; it had lost its sting a score of years ago, but his mood was still tender, and as he stared at the pile of papers on his desk, thoughts of C. & S. C. were far away. At last, however, the consciousness of this came upon him and he thought, "I reckon I need exercise," and then a moment later, "It'll be quite a trick, though, to find a horse that's up to my weight."

He had hardly taken up his work when Pease appeared and told him that a man wanted to see him. The man was a deputy sheriff, and he came to serve on James Weeks the injunction which Judge Black had signed in Porter's office two hours before.

It may be that his earlier mood had something to do with it; for as Jim laid the paper on his desk, his thoughts went back half a century to one of his boyhood days. It was a summer afternoon, and Jim and some of his friends had been in swimming; somehow it became necessary for him to fight Thomas Ransome. Jim had never been in a fight before, and he had no theories whatever, but he found that he could hit hard, and it never occurred to him to try to parry. Thomas was forced to give back steadily until his farther retreat was

cut off by the river and he saw that more vig-
orous tactics were required. With utter disre-
gard of the laws of war he drove a vicious kick
at Jim's stomach. Had it landed, its effect
would probably have been serious, but Jim, for
the first time since the fight began, stepped
back, and with both hands gave additional im-
petus to the foot, so that Thomas kicked much
higher than he had intended, and losing his balance, he toppled into the river with a very satisfactory splash.

Jim smiled at the recollection and then read
the injunction again to see if it were possible to
catch Porter's foot. His eye rested long on
the sputtery signature at the bottom, and he
thought, "I might have known that Porter
wouldn't go into this business without owning a
Judge."

He put the paper in his pocket, then locked
his desk, and with a word to Pease he left the
office. Jim dined down town, and not until
after dinner did he think of Harvey and his
leave of absence. He would need his secretary
to-morrow, and it would not do to have him out
of reach. But the moments of reminiscence
that afternoon came to Harvey's rescue, and Jim

in the most unbusinesslike way decided to get
on without his secretary. " He can't go through
that but once," thought Jim.

He left the restaurant and walked rapidly to
the Northern Station, and for the second time
that week the Northern Limited took Jim to
Manchester.

Jim was going to see Judge Grey. He had
already decided what he wanted the Judge to
do ; whether he could get him to do it was
another question, which Jim was going to put
to the test as soon as possible.

The trains on the Northern in coming into
Manchester run down the middle of one of the
main business streets, and engineers are com-
pelled by city statutes to run slowly. As the
Limited slowed down, Jim walked out on the
rear platform and stood gazing at the brightly
lighted shop windows. At an intersecting street
he saw a trolley car waiting for the train to pass ;
the blue light it showed told Jim it was the car
he wanted, so he swung quickly off the train
and stepped aboard the car as it came bumping
over the crossing. It was evidently behind its
schedule, for once on clear track again it sped
along rapidly. A man was running to catch

the car, and Jim watched him with amused interest. At first he gained, but as the speed of the car increased he gave up the race; but he had come near enough for Jim to recognize him as the man who had dined only a few tables from him that evening in Chicago and who had sat a few seats behind him on the Limited. Jim smiled. "They're mighty anxious to know what I'm doing," he thought.

Judge Grey did not go away on vacations. He was a homely man, with a large family, and he took serious views of life. He was country bred, and he had never outgrown a certain rusticity of appearance. It was said that his wife always cut his hair, and the concentric circles made by the neatly trimmed ends lent verisimilitude to the tale that she began at the crown with a butter dish to guide her scissors, then extended the diameter of her circle by using next a saucer, and last a soup bowl.

The Judge greeted Jim warmly, invited him into the library, and sat down to hear what he had to say. Jim told him almost without reservation the story of the fight for the possession of M. & T., beginning with his large investment in the road and his election to the

presidency of it. He did not try to make a
good story; he told what had happened as
simply and briefly as possible, and he interested
Judge Grey. Part of it was already known to
him, and part filled in gaps in his knowledge.
To him it was the story of an honest struggle
for something worth struggling for. When
it came to the latest move, and Jim without
comment handed him Black's injunction, the
Judge's wrath flamed out.

"That's an outrage!" he exclaimed. "It's
just a legal hold-up."

"Possibly," said Jim. "It was the best move
they could make, though. But," he went on
after a short pause, "I've got the right in this
business, and I want you to help me."

"You want me to dissolve the injunction,
I suppose," said the Judge, cautiously.

"No," said Jim. "I don't. Just the other
way. I'd like you to issue an injunction that
will go a little farther."

There was another short pause, and then
Jim began explaining his plan. As he explained and argued, the fire, which had been
crackling cheerfully when he came in, flickered
more and more faintly, and it was but a fading

glow when that most informal session of the
Circuit Court in chancery sitting came to its
conclusion.

"That's all right, then," said Jim at length,
rising as he spoke.

"Yes," said the other. "We'll do it that
way. Are you going right back to Chicago,
Mr. Weeks?"

"No," said Jim. "I shall be here for some
time. From now on this fight will be along
the line of the road."

Mr. Wing was oppressed by a sense of his
office boy's superiority. He read disapproba-
tion in the round-eyed stare, and even the cut-
steel buttons, though of Wing's own purveying,
seemed arguslike in their critical surveillance.
He would have abolished them had he not felt
that the boy would understand the change. If
the boy had only forgotten to copy letters or
had manifested an unruly desire to attend his
relatives' funerals, his employer would have
been a happier man. As it was, he felt apolo-
getic every time he came in late or went out
early.

The directors' meeting which Porter and

Thompson had decided upon on Friday was to take place the next afternoon in Wing's office; so, contrary to the little man's custom on Saturday afternoons, he returned thither after lunch.

Porter and Thompson were already there, and the former was giving the Vice-President his last instructions, with the evident purpose of stiffening him up a bit. For Thompson seemed to need stiffening badly. One by one, and two by two, the directors came straggling in, and presently Porter, with a parting injunction to Thompson, left the room and crossed over to McNally's office, where his lieutenant was waiting for him. There they plotted and planned and awaited the result of the directors' meeting across the hall.

In Wing's office the meeting was about to begin. It was easy to distinguish between Jim's friends and the C. & S. C. people; for the former, a doleful minority, were crowded in one corner doing nothing because there was nothing they could do, while on the other side of the room were the gang, with Thompson in the centre, talking in low tones over the programme of the meeting. There seemed to be no hope whatever that the President would be able to

save himself, for his opponents had a clear
majority of two, and they were met to-day to
press this advantage to the utmost. Had Jim
been there at hand, his cause would not have
seemed to his friends so desperate, for it was
hard, looking at him, to imagine him defeated;
his very bulk seemed prophetic of ultimate victory. But Jim was not there; he was not even
in Chicago.

There was one man in the minority group
who seemed somewhat less cheerless than his
companions. When they asked him what hope
there was, what way of escape he saw, he could
not answer, but he still professed to believe that
the President's downfall was not so imminent
as it seemed. And the thought that perhaps
this one man knew more than he could tell kept
the minority from becoming utterly discouraged.
The foundation for his hopes lay in a telegram
he had received that morning from Jim, which
read, " *Don't get scared, everything all right.*"
Evidently Jim was not submitting tamely, but
whatever was going to happen must happen
soon if it was not to be too late, for Thompson
was already calling the meeting to order. As
the directors seated themselves about the long

table and listened to Thompson's opening remarks, — Thompson liked to make remarks,
— it seemed that for once in his life Jim was
beaten.

At that moment, in the arched entrance to
the Dartmouth, a man whose damp forehead
and limp collar bore witness that he was in a
hurry, turned away from the wall directory he
had been scrutinizing and entered the nearest
elevator.

"Six," he said.   Once on the sixth floor he
looked about for a minute or two and walked
into the outer office where Buttons was on
guard, demanding audience with Mr. Wing.

"Mr. Wing is in," said the boy, "but he is
engaged and can't be disturbed."

"They're here, are they?" said the man.
"Well, I want to see Mr. Wing and Mr.
Thompson and Mr. Powers."

"But you can't see them," was the answer.
"There's a directors' meeting in there."

"In there, eh?" said the man, and without
further parley with Buttons, he entered the
room indicated, closing the door behind him.

Meanwhile Porter and McNally in the other
office were discussing probabilities and possi-

bilities and thinking of a good many others which neither of them cared to discuss, though all were in their way pleasant. Suddenly they were interrupted by the apparition of Buttons. His eyes were rounder than ever, and his white hair looked as though some one had tried to drag it out of his head.

"Please, sir," he gasped, "Mr. Thompson wants to see you right away."

Porter jumped to his feet and fairly ran out of the room. As he turned into the hall a muffled uproar greeted his ears, and it made him hurry the faster. But McNally stayed where he was. He, too, heard the strange noise, but he felt that he would not be able to do any good by going in there. McNally did not "come out strong" amid scenes of violence. His heart troubled him.

It was not more than five minutes before Porter came back. His face was a study.

"They're raising hell in there," he said. "Weeks's judge has just served an injunction that kicks Thompson and Wing and Powers off the board. Thompson just curled up, — he was almost too scared to breathe, — and Wing seemed to be having some sort of a fit. There was one idiot up on the table yelling that the meeting was adjourned and trying to give three cheers for Weeks." (It was the man with the telegram.)

"Well," said McNally, "what's going to happen next?"

"I don't know," said Porter, breathlessly. "I don't see that anything can happen. As things stand now there isn't a quorum of directors and all the officers are suspended. The road can't do business."

Suddenly he leaned forward in his chair and exclaimed: —

"By George, if that road doesn't need a receiver, no road ever did. Telephone Judge Black quick. We'll get in ahead of Weeks this time."

There was no delay in finding the Judge. Porter had indicated to him the advisability of keeping himself on tap, as it were, and he was now prepared to settle with neatness and despatch the legal affairs of his employers. Before dark that afternoon he had regularly and with all necessary formality appointed Frederick McNally to be receiver for the Manchester & Truesdale Railroad Company.

But it was significant of Jim Weeks's foresight that the road already had a receiver, for at that very moment he had in his pocket an order from Judge Grey appointing Harvey West to that position.

I

CHAPTER IX

THE MATTER OF POSSESSION

The M. & T. terminal station at Manchester was in reality two buildings. From the street, it looked like an ordinary three-story office building, except that there were no stores on the street level. Instead, the first floor was taken up by two large waiting rooms, the ticket office, and a baggage room. Entering through the big doorway in the centre, you ascended a few steps, passed through the waiting room, then up some more steps and across a covered iron bridge which spanned a narrow alley. This bridge connected the station proper with the train shed.

The offices of the company occupied the two upper floors. The same stairway that led to the bridge doubled on itself and zigzagged up the rest of the way. As you reached the second floor, the office of the Superintendent was before you, across the hall. To your right were large rooms occupied by various branches of the clerical force, while to your left the first door bore the word "Treasurer," and the second was lettered "President." The Treasurer's office was a large room, cut off at the rear by a vault which contained the more valuable of the company's books and papers: the main vault was downstairs. A narrow passage between the vault and the partition led to a small window which overlooked the train shed and the alley. On one side of this passage was the vault entrance, on the other was a door which had been cut through the partition into the President's private office.

Early on Monday morning, after a brief survey of the various officers and a few words with the Superintendent, Harvey assumed the direction of the road and established himself in the President's room, while a big deputy sat at the desk in the outer office. The night before, at the Illinois House, Jim and Harvey had talked until late, discussing every detail of the situation. Jim had gone over the fight of Saturday, winding up with a few words of advice.

"We'll have trouble," he said. "Porter

isn't going to let things slip away any easier than he has to. The safe plan is to suspect everything and everybody. Keep everything in sight. I'll be here to help, but from now on you represent the road."

Harvey arranged the desk to suit him, then he opened the small door behind him and crossed the passage. The vault door was open, but a steel gate barred the way. A key hung by the window, and as Harvey unlocked the gate and swung it open, a bell rang. He examined the shelves, and noted that the books were in place. He knew that the possession of those books meant practically the possession of the road.

Reëntering his office he found the deputy standing in the other doorway.

"Gentleman to see you, Mr. West," said the deputy. "Won't give his name. Says it's important."

"Show him in," Harvey replied.

The deputy stepped back and made way for a quiet-looking man who was even larger than himself. The newcomer closed the door behind him.

"Mr. West," he said, "Mr. Weeks ordered

me to report to you. I'm Mallory, from the Pinkerton agency. I have three men outside. Have you any instructions?"

Harvey checked a smile. It reminded him of the stories of his boyhood. But in a moment it dawned upon him that if Jim thought the situation so serious, he must be very careful.

"Yes," he answered slowly. "Put one man near the vault — here " — he opened the small door — "let no one go into the vault without my permission. Then you might put one man in the hall — somewhere out of sight — and one outside the building. You understand that there may be an attempt to get possession of the books. Do you know any of the C. & S. C. men — William C. Porter, or Frederick McNally?"

The detective shook his head.

"Well, then, just keep things right under your eye, and report every hour or so."

The detective nodded and left the room. A little later Harvey opened the side door, and saw a man lounging in the passage, looking idly out the window.

Shortly after ten Jim came in to talk things over. He told Harvey that the C. & S. C.

people had a counter move under way, but he was unable to discover its nature. He had seen McNally in company with a number of men who did not often leave Chicago. "He'll be up here, yet," Jim added prophetically; and he went out without leaving word. "Don't know how long I'll be gone," was all he would say; "but you'll see me off and on."

Ten minutes after Jim's departure McNally appeared. Harvey heard his voice in the outer office, then the deputy came to Harvey's desk.

"Mr. Frederick McNally," said the official. "He asked for the Superintendent first, and I sent him in to Mr. Mattison, but he sent him back to you. Will you see him?"

"Yes," replied Harvey. "And you may stay in the room."

The deputy held open the door, while McNally entered.

"How are you, West?" he said brusquely. "There seems to be some confusion here. The Superintendent disclaims all authority, and refers me to you."

"Sit down," said Harvey, waiting for McNally to continue. Evidently McNally preferred to stand.

"I wish to see some one in authority, Mr. West."

"You may talk with me."

"You — are you in authority?"

Harvey bowed, and fingered a paper-weight.

"I don't understand this, West." He glanced at the deputy. "I wish to see you alone."

For a moment Harvey looked doubtful, then he smiled slightly, and nodded at the deputy, saying, —

"Very well."

"Will you tell me what this means?" asked McNally, when the door had closed.

Harvey looked gravely at him and said nothing.

"Well?" McNally's coolness was leaving him. "Are you in control of this road, or aren't you?"

"I am."

"In that case" — he produced a paper — "it becomes my duty to relieve you."

Harvey looked at the paper; it was an order from Judge Black appointing McNally receiver for M. & T. Harvey handed it back, saying, coolly, —

"Sit down, Mr. McNally."

"I have no time to waste, West. You will please turn over the books."

"They are in the vault," said Harvey, pointing to the side door.

McNally looked sharply at Harvey, but the young man had turned to a pile of letters. After a moment's hesitation McNally opened the door and pulled at the steel gate. As he was peering through the bars, a heavy hand fell on his shoulder.

"Here!" said a low voice. "You'll have to keep away from that vault."

"Take your hand away!" McNally ordered.

"Come, now! Move on!"

"Mr. West, under whose orders is this man acting?"

"His superior officer's, I suppose," Harvey called through the door without rising.

"Call him at once, sir."

The detective beckoned to a boy, and sent him out of the room. In a moment his chief appeared.

"This man sent for you, Mr. Mallory," said the detective.

"What is it?" asked Mallory.

McNally blustered.

"I want to know what this means. Do you understand that I am the receiver of this road?"

"Oh, no, you aren't." Mallory stepped to the door. "Is this true, Mr. West?"

"No," said Harvey, "it isn't."

"You'll have to leave, then, my friend."

"Don't you touch me!" McNally's face was growing red. For reply each detective seized an arm, and the protesting receiver was hustled unceremoniously out of the room.

An hour later McNally returned. He greeted the deputy with a suave smile, and requested an interview with Mr. West.

"I'm not sure about that," said the deputy.

"That is too bad," smiled McNally. "Kindly speak to Mr. West."

With a disapproving glance the deputy opened the door. Harvey came forward.

"Well," he said brusquely, "what can I do for you?"

McNally stepped through the door and seated himself.

"I've been thinking this matter over, Mr. West, and I believe that we can come to an understanding. If your claims are correct, the road has two receivers. You are nominally in possession, but, nevertheless, you are liable for contempt of court for refusing to honor my authority. Whichever way the case is settled, I am in a position to inconvenience you for resisting me."

He waited for a reply, but Harvey waited, too.

"In the interest of the road, Mr. West, it would be very much better for you to recognize me, even to the extent of having two receivers. It could not affect the outcome of the case, and it might avoid trouble."

"I can't agree with you," Harvey replied. "I shall retain control of the road until the case is settled."

McNally rose.

"Then, I warn you, you will have a big undertaking on your hands."

"I suppose so."

"Very well; good morning."

"Good morning, Mr. McNally."

At noon Harvey went out to lunch. He met Jim at the hotel, and told him what had happened. Jim smiled at Harvey's seriousness.

"The fight hasn't begun yet," he said. "When you've been through as many deals as I have" — he stopped and drew out his watch.

"It's one-thirty. You'd better get back. I'll go with you and look over the field."

As they walked through the waiting room Harvey fancied that he heard a noise from above. However, the noon express, out in the train shed, was blowing off steam with a roar, and he could not be positive. But Jim quickened his pace, and ran up the steps with surprising agility.

As they neared the second floor the noise grew. There was scuffling and loud talking, culminating in an uproar of profanity and blows. The first man they saw was McNally. He stood near the stairway, hat on the back of his head, face red but composed. Before him was a strange scene. Mallory and the big deputy stood with their backs to the Treasurer's door, tussling with three burly ruffians. Beyond the deputy, one of the detectives was standing off two men with well-placed blows. The two other detectives were rolling about the floor, each with a man firmly in his grasp. There was a great noise of feet, as the different groups swayed and struggled. In the excitement none of them saw Jim and Harvey, who stood for a moment on the top step.

A stiff blow caught the deputy's chin, and he staggered. With a quick motion Mallory whipped out a pair of handcuffs. There was a flash of steel as he drew back his arm, then the maddened rough went down in a heap, a stream of blood flowing from his head. One of the others, a red-haired man, gripped the handcuffs and fought for them. It all happened in an instant, and as Harvey stood half-dazed, he heard a breathless exclamation, and Jim had sprung forward.

Some persons might have thought Jim Weeks fat. He weighed two hundred and forty pounds, but he was tall and wide in the shoulder. On ordinary occasions his face was so composed as to appear almost cold-blooded, but now it was fairly livid. Harvey drew in his breath with surprise; he had seen Jim angry, but never like this. In three strides Jim was behind the red-haired man. He threw an arm around the man's neck, jerking his chin up with such force that his body bent backward, and relinquishing his hold on the handcuffs he clutched, gasping, at Jim's arm. But the arm gripped like iron. While Mallory was pulling himself together and turning to aid the deputy, Jim walked backward, dragging the struggling man to the head of the stairs. On the top step he paused to grip the man's trousers with his other hand, then he literally threw the fellow downstairs. Bruised and battered, he lay for a moment on the landing, then he struggled to his feet and moved his arm toward his hip pocket, but Jim was ready. The breathless President started down the stairs with a rush. For an instant the man wavered, then he broke and fled into the train shed.

On his return Jim had to step aside to avoid another ruffian, who was walking down with profane mutterings. This time Harvey had a hand in the fighting, and he leaned over the railing to answer the man's oaths with a threat of the law. Jim and Harvey stood aside while the four detectives and the deputy led the remainder of the gang downstairs to await the police.

From the various offices frightened faces were peering through half-open doors. A few stripling clerks appeared with belated offers of assistance, but Jim waved them back. Already Jim was cooling off. He could not afford to retain such a passion, and he mopped his face and neck for a few moments without speaking. His breath was gone, but he began to recover it.

"Hello," he said, at length, "where's McNally?"

Harvey started, then ran down the hall, glancing hastily into the different offices. When he returned, Jim had vanished. While he stood irresolute, two stalwart brakemen appeared from the train shed and stood on the landing. One of them called up, —

"Can we help you, sir?"

"Wait a minute," said Harvey.

A door opened down the hall. Harvey looked toward the sound, and saw Jim backing out of the wash-room, followed by McNally, whose arm was held firmly in Jim's grasp. They came toward Harvey in silence.

"He was hiding, West," said Jim, a savage eagerness in his voice. "He hadn't the nerve to stick it out. Corker, isn't he?"

McNally stood for a moment looking doggedly out through the window over the roof of the shed.

"You've got yourself into a mess, Weeks," he said, speaking slowly in an effort to bring himself under control. "This'll land you in Joliet."

For reply Jim looked him over contemptuously, and tightened his grasp until the other winced. Then he suddenly loosened his hold, stepped back, and calling, "Catch him, boys!" kicked McNally with a mighty swing.

Harvey laughed hysterically as the flying figure sailed down the stairway, then he heard Jim say to the brakemen, —

"Take him to Mallory, and tell him to put him with the others."

"Well," said Harvey, nervously, "I guess that's settled."

"No," said Jim, "it's only just begun. He'll be on deck again before night." The next sentence was lost in the mopping handkerchief, but as he turned into the office, he added, "We'll have to lose the books to-night, West."

CHAPTER X

SOMEBODY LOSES THE BOOKS

WHEN Harvey went to dinner in the evening he left a force of ten detectives guarding the offices. Jim, who had spent the afternoon with Harvey, superintended the placing of the men. Mallory, the lieutenant in charge, was ensconced in the Superintendent's office, and six of his assistants were with him, privileged to doze until called. One man stood in the hall, in a position to watch the stairway and the windows at each end; one patrolled the waiting room; and the ninth man strolled about in front of the building, loitering in the shadows and watching the street with trained eye. Before leaving the station Jim had a short talk with Mallory.

"Watch it awful close," he said. "There's no telling what these people will do."

"Very well, Mr. Weeks. They won't get ahead of us. But I should feel a bit safer if you'd let me put a man by the vault."

Jim shook his head.

"There's such a thing as doing it too well, Mallory. And by all means I hope that you won't do that."

He looked closely at the detective, who glanced away with a cautious nod.

That evening after dinner, Jim telephoned for Mattison, the Superintendent, and a long talk ensued in Jim's room at the hotel. Neither he nor Harvey wasted time in recounting the experiences of the day; they had too many plans for the night. As Jim had said, it was necessary to lose the books, and to lose them thoroughly. It was equally important that the action should not be confided to any ordinary employee. The fewer men that knew of it, the safer Jim would be, and so he finally decided to confine the information within its original limits.

"You two are lively on your feet," he said. "And it is a good deal better for you to do it."

"How about the detectives?" asked Mattison.

"You'll have to keep out of their way. Mallory won't trouble you so long as you keep still; but remember, every man, detective or

K

not, that catches you, makes one more chance for evidence against us."

"But isn't the building surrounded?"

"No. There's only one man outside, and he is in front. You can go through the alley and climb up to the window — it's only the second floor. Mallory has orders to keep out of the vault room. He's over in your office, Mattison."

"I suppose," suggested Harvey, "that unless we are actually caught with the books, we can throw a bluff about a tour of inspection or something of that sort."

"And if we are caught," said Mattison, "I suppose we can run like the devil."

"You'll have to trust the details more or less to circumstances," was Jim's reply.

"How about the books?" asked Harvey. "What shall we do with them?"

"Mattison had better take care of them. We can't bring them to the hotel, and anyhow, it is just as well if you and I, West, don't know anything about them. Then, when we want them again, it is a good deal easier for Mattison to find them than for any one else. Sort of accident, you know."

It was finally agreed that before attempting to get the books, Harvey and Mattison should make a *bona fide* tour of inspection, by this means finding out where each man was located. Mattison reminded them that the watchman in the train shed was not to be overlooked, but they decided to chance him.

"There's one thing about it," said Mattison, smiling. "If Johnson doesn't catch us, I can discharge him for incompetency."

Shortly after midnight Harvey and Mattison started out. They found the station dark. As they tiptoed slowly along, edging close to the building, everything was silent. They reached the arched doorway, and were turning in when the glare of a bull's-eye lantern flashed into their eyes. Mattison laughed softly.

"That's business," he said.

"What are you up to?" growled the man behind the lantern.

"Where's Mallory?" was Mattison's answer.

The man hesitated, then whistled softly. The whistle was echoed in the waiting room. In a few moments the door opened and a voice said, "What's up?"

"Two chaps want Mallory."

Harvey and Mattison still stood on the stone step, looking into the lantern. They could see neither door nor man. After a short wait, evidently for scrutiny, the door closed. When it opened again, Mallory's voice said, " Close that light," adding, " Is anything the matter, Mr. West ? "

" No," replied Harvey. " We're keeping an eye open. I see your men know their business. Have you had any trouble ? "

" Everything is quiet. Do you care to come in ? "

Harvey responded by entering, with Mattison following. As they crossed the waiting room, Mallory drew their attention to a shadow near a window.

" One of our boys," he said in a low tone. " I put out all the lights. It makes it a good deal easier to watch."

Up in Mattison's office the detectives were lounging about, some dozing, some conversing in low tones. The gas burned low, and the window shutters were covered with the rugs from the 'President's office, to keep the light from the street.

The two officials, after a glance about the

room, returned to the hall. Harvey tried the door of each office, then returned to Mattison and Mallory. While they stood whispering, — for at night sound travels through an empty building, — there came the sound of a window sliding in its sash, apparently from the Treasurer's office.

Mallory paused to listen, then coolly turned and continued the conversation.

"What was that?" muttered Harvey.

The lieutenant affected not to hear the remark.

"Some one is getting into the building," Harvey whispered. Mattison stepped lightly across the hall and, bending down, listened at the keyhole. He returned with an excited gesture.

"Don't you hear it?" he asked.

"No," said Mallory. "I don't hear anything."

"Are you deaf, man?"

"No, but I think I know when to hear."

It occurred to Harvey that Jim had done his work well. But then, Jim's orders, however brief, were always understood. Harvey motioned the others to be silent, and tiptoed across the floor. He listened as Mattison had done, then passed on to the President's door. Cautiously he drew a bunch of keys from his pocket, and feeling for the right one he slipped it into the lock, threw open the door, and darted into the office. Mattison and the detective followed, stumbling over chairs, and colliding with the door to the inner office, which had closed after Harvey. In the dim light they could see two figures struggling in the passage by the vault. While Mattison sprang forward, Mallory quickly lighted the gas.

The light showed that Harvey had crowded the fellow up against the vault door. The new-comer was a medium-sized man, rough-faced, and poorly clad. On the floor was a small leather grip, which evidently had been kicked over in the scuffle, for part of a burglar's kit was scattered about the passage.

Mallory jerked the man's wrists together, slipped on the handcuffs, and led him out into the hall. In a moment the detective returned.

" I left him with the boys, for the present. Case of common safe-cracking."

" Do you think so?" said Harvey, adjusting his cuffs, and moving the strange tools with his foot. "If he wanted money, I should think he would have tackled the vault downstairs."

Mallory stooped, and replaced the kit in the bag. Suddenly he said, —

"Raise your foot, Mr. West."

Harvey did so, and the detective arose with a dirty paper in his hand. He looked it over, and handed it to the others. It was a rough pencil sketch of the station building, showing the alley, the window, the Treasurer's office, and the vault.

"What do you think of it?" asked Mallory.

Harvey turned it over. A second glance showed it to be the front of an envelope, for part of an end flap remained. The upper left-hand corner had been torn off, evidently to remove the return card, but so hastily that a part of the card remained. Straightening it out, and holding it up to the light, Harvey read : —

———esleigh,
———ster, Illinois.

Mallory looked over his shoulder, and exclaimed : —

"That's easy. Hotel Blakesleigh, Manchester, Illinois."

"How does that help you?" asked Mattison.

Harvey lowered the paper.

"Don't you see," he replied. "There are two good hotels here, the Illinois and the Blakesleigh. McNally is not at the Illinois." He turned to the detective. "You'd better let the fellow go, Mallory."

"Why?"

"Because it is the easiest way to handle it. Keep the tools, though."

"But I don't understand, Mr. West."

"Well, there is no use in discussing it. We won't prefer charges."

"But the man was caught in the act."

"He didn't get anything, poor devil. No; we're after bigger game than this. We have enough for evidence. And don't sweat him."

"This is too deep for me, Mr. West. Surely there's no harm in questioning him, now that I've got him."

"Can't help it, Mallory. When that man reports to his employer, I want him to say that we suspect nothing beyond his attempt to crack the safe."

The detective turned away with a frown.

"I suppose you know your business, Mr. West."

Harvey and Mattison followed him to the

hall, closing the door after them. They said good night, and left the building.

"See here, West," said Mattison, when they were fairly around the corner, "wasn't that a little hasty? It wouldn't hurt to keep the man out of the way."

"No, I don't agree with you. What McNally has done so far will be upheld by his judge. And another thing, Mattison; just at present, it isn't to our interest to get an investigation under way. We're going to do the same thing ourselves."

Slowly and cautiously they slipped around the next square, and, by returning through the alley, brought up in the shadow of a building, across the street from the train shed. Here they waited to reconnoitre. The night was clear, and the arc-lamp at the corner threw an intermittent glare down the street. As they looked, a long shadow appeared on the sidewalk. Mattison gripped Harvey's arm, and drew him back into the alley. They crouched behind a pile of boxes.

"It's like stealing apples," whispered Harvey. "When the old man gets after you with a stick."

"Ssh!"

The footsteps sounded loud on the stone walk. Then a helmeted figure passed the alley, and went on its way.

Waiting until the sound died in the distance, the two stepped to the walk, looked hastily toward each corner, and ran across the street. Once in the station alley, they paused again.

"Look!" said Harvey, pointing; "he left the ladder."

Sure enough, a light ladder reached from the ground nearly to a second-story window, which stood open.

"Well, here we are," Mattison whispered. "How do you feel?"

"First-class. Better let me go, — I know the combination."

Mattison stood at the foot of the ladder, and steadied it while Harvey stealthily climbed to the window. Drawing himself into the passage, the receiver set to work on the vault lock. He turned the knob very slowly, guarding against the slightest noise, but the faint light that came through the window was not enough to bring out the numbers. Harvey leaned back and considered. The scratching of a match would almost surely be heard by the detectives. He leaned out the window, and beckoned. Mattison came creeping up, and Harvey explained in a few whispered sentences. "Go back and look up the street," he concluded. "We've got to light it outside the building."

While Mattison was gone, Harvey felt his way through the Treasurer's office and paused to listen; then he drew up a chair which stood near the door, and climbing up, slipped off his coat and hung it over the half-open transom. Then he closed the transom, and the room was practically light proof. With the same caution he reached the floor, and tiptoed back to the window, where he found Mattison waiting on the ladder.

"All right," whispered the Superintendent. "Are you ready?"

"Yes."

Mattison struck a match on his trousers leg, shielded it with his hands, then handed it to Harvey, who kneeled at the door and began to whirl the knob. Before he was through the light was close to his fingers, and he held another match to the flame, taking care to light the wrong end. At last the lock clicked, and Harvey opened the door a few inches, then he whispered to Mattison, "If I whistle, you get down and I'll drop the books."

He swung the door open, but stopped bewildered. Before him was the steel gate with the clanging bell. However, the risk must be run, so motioning Mattison to climb down he drew out his keys, and with a match ready in his hand he jerked the gate open and dashed into the vault. Striking the match, he quickly located the books he needed, carried them to the window and pitched them out. Then he heard a thud on the door. He threw one leg over the sill, but stopped — his coat was still on the transom. Some one was struggling to break in the door now, for it shook. Harvey sprang back, mounted the chair, and tore down his coat, tumbling to the floor, chair and all, with a clatter. A voice shouted, "Open the door, or I'll shoot!" but Harvey gave no heed. He ran to the window and literally fell down the ladder, filling his hands with slivers. There came a crash from above, and a muttered oath, and Harvey knew that the door had given way. He gave the ladder a shove, and as it fell upon the cobblestones with a great noise, he turned and sped up the alley after a dark figure that was already near to the corner.

He caught up with Mattison in the next block, and relieved him of half the load. Then for a long time they ran and doubled, fugitives from half a dozen detectives and a few lumbering policemen. At last Mattison turned up a dark alley in the residence district. Coming to a board fence, he threw the books over, then climbed after. Harvey followed, and found himself on a tennis court. Mattison led the way through the yard, past a dark house, and across the street to a roomy frame residence.

"Come in with me," he said to Harvey. "You can't go back to the hotel now."

Harvey laughed nervously and nodded. Mattison opened the door with his night key, and with the heavy books in their arms the two burglars stole up to bed.

CHAPTER XI

A POLITICIAN

Any man whose interests are extensive and diverse has sooner or later to master the art of making other men work for him, and he must be content to trust the management of a great part of his affairs to other hands. Jim Weeks loved to keep a grasp even on the comparatively insignificant details of his business, but he showed wonderful insight in the selection of his lieutenants, and he could impart such momentum to his projects that they moved forward as he meant them to, though his own hand was not guiding them. Like other men accustomed to giving orders, he took it for granted that his directions would be carried out.

Bridge, the Tillman City alderman to whom he had intrusted the task of watching Blaney, had worked for Jim long enough to know that this affair was in his own hands, and that something more than obedience and zeal was expected of him. Though Jim's words had been brief, it was easy to see that the matter was important; important enough to give Bridge a great opportunity. He wanted to make the most of it, and, in the excitement of laying his plans, the design for the stable was forgotten.

As the day wore on and his scheme crystallized, he fluctuated between a sort of exalted confidence and the depths of nervous depression. He was naturally a steady, humdrum sort of man, but he was planning to do an audacious thing. His chance had come, and he meant to take it. At last, just before supper time, he resolutely locked his office, and started out to see Blaney. He hesitated a second or two before the contractor's house; then he ran up the steps and rang the bell.

The door was opened by a little girl, who peered up at him through the dusk with a child's curiosity. Bridge knew her, but he was of that kind of bachelors who are embarrassed in the presence of children.

"Good evening, Louise," he said. "Is your father home?"

"No, sir, he isn't," she answered.

There was a moment of awkward silence, and then he stammered, —

"Well — good night." He bent down and gravely shook hands with her, and turned to go down the steps, but at that moment Blaney himself appeared.

"How are you?" he said. "Did you want to see me?"

"If you've got the time," said Bridge.

Blaney led the way into the house, and motioned Bridge to a seat in the parlor. He himself paused in the hall to swing Louise up to his shoulder and down again.

"What's the matter with you to-night?" he asked. "You don't seem to want to play. Are you sick?"

"A little," answered the child. "I'm kind of tired, and my head hurts."

He ran his thick hand through her red curls, and looked at her anxiously for a moment. Then he followed Bridge into the parlor.

"What can I do for you, Bridge?" he asked gruffly.

Bridge hesitated a moment; then he said, "Jim Weeks was in town this morning."

Blaney looked up sharply, and asked, "Did you see him?"

"Yes," answered the other. "That is, he came down to see me. You know the M. & T. election is coming pretty soon now, and he got the idea that our stock was going to be voted against him. He wanted me to fix it up so things would go his way in the Council, and I told him that I'd do what I could. I came around to you to see if your crowd were going to do anything about it."

The coolness of the inquiry almost stupefied Blaney, but he managed to speak.

"I'd like to know," he said, "what business that is of yours, anyway."

"It's my business, right enough," said Bridge, easily. "I could ask the same question in Council meeting, but I thought it was best to talk it over with you quietly. There isn't any good in trying to fight Jim Weeks, and I should think you'd know it. If ever a man had a cinch — "

"What are you up to, anyhow?" demanded Blaney, now thoroughly exasperated. "Did you come around here to try to bulldoze me? Well, I'll just tell you you may as well save your breath. Do you understand that? Weeks thinks he can come his old bluff down here,

L

but he's going to get fooled just once. We've got the backing that'll beat him. That's all I've got to say to you."

"Well, I've got a little more to say to you," said Bridge. "I came around here on my own hook to find out whether you were just making your regular bluff or whether you meant to fight, and I've found out. And now I'm going to give you your choice. I'll either give you the hottest scrap you ever had, and make what I can out of Weeks by it, or I'll go in with you so you can get your deal through quietly. You can take your choice."

"What the devil do you mean?"

"I mean just this. That if there's any possible show of kicking that damned bully out of here so that he'll never come back, I'd like to be in it. And I guess my services would be valuable."

"Look here," demanded Blaney, sharply. "What have you got against Weeks?"

"What have I got against him?" repeated Bridge. His face was flushed and his shining eyes and clenched hands testified to his excitement. "Hasn't he made me pull his hot chestnuts off the fire for the last two years? Hasn't

he held me up and made me pay a good rake-
off from every deal I've been lucky enough to
make a little on? And hasn't he loaned me
money until I don't dare sign my own name
without asking him if I can do it, and —" He
stopped as though knowing he had gone too
far; then he laughed nervously. "It's all
right what I've got against him; that's my
business, I guess, but —"

Again the unfinished sentence was eloquent.

This time it was Blaney who broke the
silence. " I guess," he said cautiously, "that if
you want to tip Weeks over, you'll find there'll
be some to help you."

Bridge laughed bitterly. "There are plenty
who'd be glad enough to do it if they could.
He's had his grip on all of us long enough for
that; but I'm afraid it's no good. We can't
beat him. He's got us in a vise."

" I don't know about that," said Blaney.

"Why, man," exclaimed the other, "what
can we do? And if we try to buck him and get
left, he'll squeeze the life out of us. You know
that."

Blaney did know that, and Bridge's words
brought certain unpleasant consequences plainly

before his mind. All the while Bridge was talking Blaney had been trying to find out what his motive was. He had always believed that Bridge was hand and glove with Weeks, and at the beginning he had suspected a trap. But what Bridge had said was entirely plausible ; he had given himself away without reserve, and had frankly confessed that Weeks had been driving him. Bridge would be a valuable ally in the scheme Blaney wanted to put through. Jim was popular in Tillman, and if he were to be sold out to a corporation like C. & S. C., it would, as Bridge had hinted, be well for all parties concerned in the transfer that it should be accomplished as quietly as possible. Bridge was at the head of a compact and determined minority, and if he opposed the deal, he could make matters very uncomfortable for Blaney and his henchmen. But with Bridge on his side the field was clear and there could be no doubt as to the success of the scheme. The one thing that troubled Blaney was that Bridge might demand money ; but there was no need of facing that issue yet, for Bridge had apparently not thought of it. "He's just getting even for something," thought Blaney.

There was a long silence, which Blaney broke at last.

"We don't have to buck him all by ourselves," he said. "We're well backed. C. & S. C. are behind us. Are you with us?"

Bridge answered him steadily. "I've been waiting for a chance like this for a year," he said. "You can count me in for all I'm worth."

He rose to go and held out his hand to Blaney. "Good night," he said, "and good luck to us."

"So long," was the answer. "I'll come around in a day or two, and we can.arrange details."

The interview had been a hard one for Bridge, and it left him weak and nervous. When he sat down to supper at his boarding-house table that evening he had no appetite. He went to bed early, but he did not sleep well, and the next morning found him exhausted by the interminable hours of dozing, uneasy half-consciousness. He spent the next day in hoping that Blaney would come, though he had no reason for expecting him so soon, and by night he was in worse condition than ever. He would have gone again to see Blaney had he dared, but he felt that such a proceeding would imperil the whole affair; he must wait for Blaney to make the next move.

Day followed day with no variation save that Bridge found the delay more and more nearly unbearable, and the week had dragged to an end and another begun before anything happened. On Sunday afternoon he started out for a walk, but he had not gone far when he met Blaney. To his surprise, the contractor looked as though the past week had been as hard for him as it had been for Bridge. His face looked thin and his eyes sunken and there were bristling uneven patches of sandy beard on his face. When he came up to Bridge he stopped.

"I suppose you've been looking for me," he said. "I've been staying right at home taking care of my kid; she's had the scarlet fever."

"Louise?" asked Bridge, with real concern. "I hope she's better."

"I guess she'll pull through all right now," answered Blaney, "but she's been pretty sick, and it's kept me busy night and day. You see my wife can't do much at nursing. But I tell you scarlet fever is no joke."

"I never had it," was the answer, "but I'm

glad it's come out all right. By the way," he went on, as Blaney started to walk away, "when will you be able to talk over that business with me?"

"Why, now as well as at any time, I suppose," said Blaney, after a moment's hesitation.

The contractor had an office near by, and at his suggestion they went there for their conference.

"How many men can you count?" he asked when they were seated.

Now that the period of forced inaction was over, and there was something important to do, Bridge forgot that his head was burning and his throat dry, and for the first time in three days he was able to think consecutively. For half an hour they figured their united strength and talked over the individual members of the Council. But at last Bridge said : —

"Before we go any further, I want to know more about this business. I've taken your word so far that we would be backed up all right, and I hope we are. But I can't afford to be beaten, and if Weeks isn't clean busted up, he'll hound me to death. I've got to know more about this business."

Blaney looked out of the window. " Seems

to me you're pretty late with that talk about not going in," he said.

"I know I've committed myself to some extent without knowing just what I was getting into," answered Bridge, "but I won't go any farther till some things are cleared up."

"What do you want to know?" asked Blaney.

"I want to know what you're going to do. Voting that stock against Weeks won't do any good. We can't get him out all by ourselves."

"We aren't all by ourselves. C. & S. C. are with us."

"That's what I'm trying to get at. To what extent are they with us?"

Blaney hesitated. It had not been a part of his plan to tell of the prospective sale of the stock. He had meant to have the Council direct the voting of the stock for C. & S. C. faction, and then when they had committed themselves by this act, to urge upon them the necessity of selling out and to tempt them with the offer of par. But a glance at Bridge's set face convinced him that the new ally meant what he said, and he knew too much already for the safety of the scheme unless he were further-ing it.

"They're with us to this extent," said Blaney, slowly. "They're going to buy our stock."

"That's all rot," said Bridge. "We can't sell. M. & T.'s a good investment now, and it's getting better every day."

"Wait till I get through," interrupted Blaney, bent now on making an impression. "Don't you think the Council would vote to sell at par?"

"What's that got to do with it?"

"C. & S. C. are going to pay par, that's all."

Bridge looked at him incredulously. "Then we're to vote the stock as they dictate, just on the strength of their telling us they'll pay par for it afterward. I'm afraid it'll be a long time afterward. How do you know they aren't play-ing us for suckers?"

"How do we know?" repeated Blaney. "I'm not quite as green as you think. I know because I've got it down in black and white. They can't get around a contract like that."

Unlocking a drawer in his desk, he drew out a sheet of paper which he thrust into Bridge's hands. "Read it," he said.

Bridge read it through once and then again;

it was briefly worded, and he had no difficulty in remembering it.   As he laid the paper down he was conscious of a violent throbbing in his head, and he shivered as though an icy breeze had blown upon him.   He rose uncertainly from his chair and moved toward the door.

"What's the matter?" demanded Blaney. "Where are you going?"

"I don't feel very well," said Bridge.   "I think I'll go home and go to bed."

When he reached the foot of the stairs, however, he turned not toward his room, but toward the railway station; for in his mind there was a confused purpose of going to Chicago immediately and telling Jim Weeks exactly what he had found out.

Scarlet fever is not ordinarily a man's disease, but it had fallen upon Bridge.   He had exposed himself to it on the evening when he went to Blaney's house to make the preliminary move in his game; and now after the five days of tense inaction it attacked him furiously.

He was in a raging fever when he left Blaney's office, but he did not realize it, borne up as he was by the excitement of winning.   There could be no doubt that he had done as good a stroke

of work for himself as for Jim Weeks, for Jim
was not the man to let the merit of his lieutenants go unrecognized. He felt sure that Jim
would win the fight, even with C. & S. C. against
him, and though he had not recognized the worthlessness of the contract Blaney held, he was confident that Jim could use his knowledge of the
existence of such a contract with telling effect.

As he walked on, the exhilaration of his tri-
umph died out of him, and his steps faltered
and his sight became untrustworthy. He realized that he was not fit for travelling, and reluctantly he turned back to his room. He was a
long time in reaching it, and when he staggered
in and dropped into an easy-chair he knew that
he was a very sick man. With a foreboding
of the delirium that was coming upon him he
gathered himself together for a final effort and
scrawled a copy of the contract upon a slip of
paper. With shaking hands he folded it and
crammed it into an inner pocket; then he rose
and moved slowly toward the bed. He fell
twice in the short distance, but he kept on, and
his head sank back in the pillows before consciousness forsook him.

CHAPTER XII

KATHERINE

As Katherine drove home alone on Sunday morning she was troubled. In aiding Harvey to catch the train for Manchester she had acted upon the veriest impulse, and Katherine liked to imagine herself a very cool and self-possessed young woman. Slowly it dawned upon her that by helping Harvey she had set her hand against her own father. In an impersonal way she had realized this, but Harvey's presence had filled her thoughts, and she had not allowed herself time to consider. And now that the cooler after-thoughts had come she was almost as indignant with herself for showing such open interest in Harvey as for hurting her father's cause. Then she grew startled to realize that even in her thoughts she was placing this man before her father. Harvey was not a fool. He would see that she had been disloyal, and he would cease to respect her. She wondered if she was disloyal.

On reaching home she hurried to her room and sat down by the open window, looking out over the lawn that sloped down to the road. Harvey would think her weak, and would feel that he could sway her from her strongest duty.

The day was bright. Far in the distance she could see a bend of the river. There was no sound, no life; the rolling country stretched away in idle waves, the checkered farms lay quiet in the sun, over all was the calm of a country Sunday. Her eyes wandered and she closed them, resting her fingers on the lids. Life was serious to Katherine. Since her early teens she had lived without a mother, and the result of her forced independence was a pronounced and early womanhood. She had learned her lessons from experience and had learned them with double force. She had never been in love, and save for a very few youthful flutterings had never given the idea a concrete form; and now that she should manifest such weakness before Harvey partly alarmed her. She suspected that he loved her, but would not permit herself to return it. She knew too little

about him, and, besides, her first duty was with
her father.   She had yielded to impulse, but it
was not too late to reconsider.   She had aided
the enemy by a positive act; she would do as
much for her father.   With firm eyes she rose
and went downstairs, fully decided to investigate the matter until she could discover a
means of throwing her energy against Weeks
and Harvey.

During the next two days her determination
grew.   Mr. Porter was in Chicago and Manchester, and was not expected home immediately, so Katherine had plenty of time for
thinking.   She drove a great deal, went around
the links every morning, and tried to read.   It
did not occur to her that her effort was not so
much to side with her duty as to crowd down
the thoughts of Harvey that would steal into
her mind.   She permitted herself no leeway in
the matter, but kept resolutely to her decision.

Tuesday afternoon she drove until quite late,
and returning found her father and McNally
awaiting dinner.   Although she was quicker
than usual in her efforts to entertain their
guest, the meal was hurried and uncomfortable.
When in repose McNally's face was clouded,

and the occasional spells of interest into which he somewhat studiously aroused himself could not conceal his general inattention. Her father, too, was preoccupied, and was so abrupt in his conversation as to leave small trace of the easy lightness of manner that Katherine had always known.

After dinner Katherine excused herself, and stepped out through the long window that opened on the veranda. Evidently a crisis had come, and she wished that an opportunity would arise through which she might join their discussion. Just outside of the library window she sat down on a steamer chair and gazed up at the dark masses of the trees, the thinning tops of which were at once darkened and relieved by the last red of the western sky.

"Yes, Porter, they kicked me out. My men and I made a stiff fight for it, but they outnumbered us."

At the sound of McNally's voice Katherine started guiltily. It had not occurred to her that the matter would be discussed downstairs; usually her father's private conversations were held in his den on the second floor. She wondered whether she ought to make herself known.

Then she heard McNally again, answering a low-spoken question from her father.

" He was a good man, or perhaps you would call him a bad one. He was just getting down to work on the vault door when West and his gang of Pinkertons broke in on him and nailed him."

Another question from Porter.

" No, Porter, they are on to us now. You see, the books are gone, and there's no use in trying to get hold of that end of the road ; but we can seize it from this end and get everything except their building."

With cheeks burning and with conscience troubling, Katherine rose and stood before the window.

" I didn't intend to put myself in your way," she said, laughing nervously, "but I couldn't help hearing."

Looking in through the dim light Katherine thought she saw McNally start. After a brief but embarrassing pause Porter spoke, using the tone Katherine associated with the stern but kindly rebukes of her childhood.

" Did you hear all we said, Katherine ? "

" Most of it, I'm afraid."

"You understand, dear, that this is very confidential business?"

"Yes, dad." With an impulsive start Katherine seated herself on the low sill of the window and clasped her hands in her lap. "I wish you would let me talk it over with you. You know I am interested in your affairs, dad. And," hesitatingly, "maybe I can help you."

For a space all three were silent. Katherine was leaning back in a pose that brought out all her unconscious beauty. The waning light fell full upon her, and the sunset seemed to be faintly reflected in her face. Her hair was coiled above her forehead in easy disorder.

McNally, sitting back in the shadow, looked fixedly at her, and as he looked it seemed to him that her beauty spiced the atmosphere. He found himself drawing in his breath keenly and almost audibly, and gripping the arms of the easy-chair : with a sudden half-amused feeling of boyishness he relaxed his grip and leaned back comfortably. It was some time since the introspective Mr. McNally had found it necessary to reprove himself for such a slip of demeanor.

"I couldn't help seeing what was going on,"

M

continued Katherine. "And you told me the other day that I had helped you some." She turned appealingly toward her father, who sat with head lowered, scowling at the carpet. McNally broke the pause.

"There is very little we can tell you, Miss Katherine. A business matter of this importance is too complicated for any one who has not grown up with the problems. It would involve the history of two railroads for years back."

"Why is it," asked Katherine, earnestly, "that a man never credits a woman with common sense? I am not blind. I know that the M. & T. is a feeder to C. & S. C., that it supplies us with coal, and that we could earn and save money by making it a part of our system. Mr. Weeks is fighting us for some reason, and we are planning to force the question. Isn't that so?"

"Where did you learn this, Katherine?" asked her father.

"From no one particular source. You have told me a great deal yourself, dad."

"The question is, Miss Katherine," McNally said, "what good could you possibly do? Without implying any doubt of your ability, you see our course is already mapped out for us by circumstances. In fact, there is only one way open that leads to a logical outcome. If we were in a position where we needed tactful advice, you could undoubtedly be of help, but just now what we want is a force of strong, aggressive men."

"Mr. McNally is right, dear," said Porter. "Everything is decided, and all we can do is to tend to business. This Weeks is following rather a dishonorable course, and we are prepared to meet him; that is all."

Katherine leaned forward and twisted the curtain string around her finger.

"Is he really dishonest?" she asked.

"Well, dear, that is a hard question. No man has a right to condemn another without careful deliberation; but it happens that many business dealings savor a little of underhand methods, and it looks to us as though Mr. Weeks were not over particular."

"What has he done?"

"Well, you see, dear —"

Katherine broke in with unusual warmth. "Oh, I know what you are going to say. Some more complications that I couldn't understand. Why won't you tell me?"

Porter arose.

"We'll talk this over at some other time, Katherine. I have an appointment with Judge Black for this evening, but I will be back before long." He added to McNally, "He came in on the 8.25. I'll leave you with Katherine."

When he had gone there was a silence. Katherine felt that her father's absence should alter the tone of the conversation, but she waited for McNally to take the initiative.

"What a glorious night," he said at length, rising and coming to the window. "Did you ever see such a lingering afterglow? Suppose we sit outside."

Katherine rose and made room for McNally to step through the open window. Together they walked across the veranda, McNally seating himself on the railing, Katherine leaning against one of the stone columns.

"How long have you been ambitious to be a business woman, Miss Katherine?"

"I hardly wish that. Only I like to share father's interests."

"Do you know, I like it. I like to see a woman show an independent interest in important affairs. Nowadays not only young girls but women of position seem to care for nothing but the frivolous. I don't know but what our pioneer ancestors got more out of life, when the woman and her husband worked side by side."

"Will you tell me about the M. & T. business, Mr. McNally?"

"I hardly feel that I can, Miss Katherine. To my mind that rests with your father."

"Probably it does, but father still thinks me a child. He thinks I cannot grasp the situation."

"Even if I felt at liberty to discuss it, I don't know what I could tell you beyond a mere recital of dry detail. Personally, I should like to do so, Miss Katherine; I honestly admire your independence, and I believe that you might even be able to suggest some helpful ideas, but business does not concern itself with the personal equation."

Katherine looked thoughtfully at McNally's shadowed face. She was a little surprised with herself that she should so persist, but it did not occur to her to stop. Deep behind her desire to be honest with her father was a desire to prove that Harvey was, after all, in the right. She did not recognize this, she did not even know it, but Harvey's personality had taken on hers a vital grip that was as yet too strong, too firm, too close at hand to be realized. As for McNally, his intention to evade was too evident to be overlooked. He was dodging at every turn, and it was becoming clear to her that he was concealing facts which it would not do to disclose. And this suggested that her father was doing the same. The bit of conversation she had overheard came back to her, and as she thought it over it sounded odder than when she had first heard it. Why should her father wish to seize the road? If it belonged to Mr. Weeks, and if he did not care to sell, what right had her father or any one else to take it by force? She had been looking out over the lawn, but now she turned and fixed her eyes intently on McNally's plump, smooth-shaven face. He was looking toward her, but seemed not to see her. Instead there was the shadow of a smile in his eyes which suggested air-castles.

"Mr. McNally," she said abruptly, "if we want the M. & T. road, why don't we buy it and pay for it?"

McNally started. During the long silence he had been feasting on Katherine's beauty. He was not a young man, but as he gazed at the earnest young face before him, and at the masses of shining hair, half in shadow, half in light, he felt a sudden loneliness, a sudden realization of what such a woman could be to him, what an influence she might have upon his life. And losing for the moment the self-poise that was his proudest accomplishment, Mr. McNally stammered.

"Oh," he said, "we couldn't—it wouldn't do—"

From the change in every line of Katherine's pose he knew that he had said enough. She had turned half away from him and was standing rigid, looking out into the night. Glancing at her dimly outlined profile, McNally could see that her lips were pressed closely together. He pulled himself together and stood up.

"Why not go in and have some music?" he asked. "This conversation is too serious for such an evening."

Katherine bowed and led the way into the house. As they passed through the library toward the piano she paused to turn the electric-light key. With the flood of light Katherine's ease returned, and she laughed lightly as she pointed to a gaudily decorated sheet of music on the piano.

"Shocking, isn't it?" she said. "That's the kind of music we play down here in the country. We need your influence to keep us from degenerating musically. Play me something good."

McNally glanced at her with a laugh.

"Coon songs, eh?" he replied. "Well, some of them aren't so bad." He sat down at the instrument and let his hands slip over the keys. Katherine sank upon the broad couch in the corner. She was apparently her old self, friendly and interested in Mr. McNally and his music, but there was nevertheless a distinct change. McNally felt the difference and tried to throw it off, but the force of the situation grew upon him. Slowly he realized that in spite of her pretensions she was not really in sympathy either with him or with her father. He struck into a Liszt rhapsody with all the fervor he could muster.

McNally was a good musician. He possessed the power, lacking in many better pianists, of using music as a medium to connect his own and his listener's moods; but to-night he fell

short, and he knew it.   He stole a glance at
Katherine.   She looked exactly as usual, but
still there was a difference that baffled him.
He threw all his art into the music.   He
labored to color it with sincerity and strength.
But all the while he knew that the ground was
lost.   What he did not know was that Katherine was passing through a crisis, and that her
thoughts were miles away from him and his
rhapsody.   He ended with unusual brilliancy,
and she smiled with pleasure and thanked him
simply, but still he felt the change.   Then Porter came in, and after a brief general conversation Katherine withdrew.

She did not go at once to her room.   Instead,
she slipped out on the little second-floor bal-
cony and sat down to be alone and to think.
She had made an honest effort to throw her
interest with her father and with what she
believed to be her duty, and now that the evening was gone she had nothing to show for it.
For a very few moments she wondered at it
all, and at the fate which seemed to draw her
toward Harvey.   Then, as the thought of him
again took concrete form, and as the last two
days with him came back to her mind, her

whole heart went out to him, and she was startled, frightened at the strength of his hold upon her. For a moment she gave herself up to dreams, dreams of a better, sweeter existence than any she had dared to imagine, then came the thought of her father, and Katherine broke down.

Downstairs, McNally and Porter sat for a long time with only a desultory conversation. Then McNally said, —

"Porter, I envy you a daughter like that."

"She is a good girl," Porter replied.

CHAPTER XIII

TRAIN NO. 14

THE fight for the possession of the Manchester and Truesdale Railroad divides itself naturally into two acts. During the first week, while it would be absurd to say that the acts of either side were legal, all the proceedings had worn the cloak of law. But now matters had come to a deadlock. Judge Grey was both able and willing to undo any or all of the acts of Judge Black, and conversely. The last event of the first act was the attempt on Tuesday morning of the C. & S. C. people, armed with writs from Black, to seize the books of the company. They were courteously received and the vaults were thrown open to their inspection; but as the books had been spirited away the night before, the search was fruitless. Porter and McNally had been beaten at their own game, and they withdrew their forces to Truesdale. The fight was to be kept up on other lines.

Wednesday morning, No. 7 on the C. & S. C. brought down a much larger number of passengers for Truesdale than ordinarily came on that train. They climbed down to the station platform from different cars, and regarded each other with studied indifference, but there was something homogeneous about the crowd that drew upon it the frankest stares of the station loafers. There were no women or children among them, they carried no baggage, and there was an air about them, carefully repressed but still discernible, which suggested that if any one were looking for trouble they were the men to whom to apply. They seemed to be trying to attract as little attention as possible, but they were followed by many curious glances, as they straggled in a long irregular line up the street toward the Truesdale Hotel.

Katherine had driven into town that morning, and from her high trap she watched the spectacle with amused interest. Seeing McNally coming out of the hotel office she pulled up her horses and nodded to him with a peremptory cordiality which left him no escape from coming to speak to her.

"So war is declared," she said laughingly, nodding toward the rear guard who were disappearing in the hotel entrance. "I see you are massing your troops. Is that the entire army, or only a division?"

McNally tried to utter a protest, but she went on unheeding. "I think they're too absurdly comical for words. They try so hard to look as if they weren't spoiling for a fight."

"Miss Porter," said McNally, seriously, "your father's interests are at stake now and we must be discreet."

"I suppose so," she said; "but really those men are irresistibly funny."

She gathered up the reins and the horses started, but as they moved away she turned and called back to him, —

"Be sure and come out to luncheon — that is, if you don't go to the front."

The words troubled McNally. Only two days before he had been dragged out of his hiding-place in the Manchester station and kicked downstairs. This experience still occupied a large place in his thoughts, and he

took Katherine's remark as a reflection on his
personal courage. Though he had no idea
of " going to the front," he decided not to go
to the Porters' for luncheon.

All that morning new people kept streaming
into Truesdale. No. 22 brought in McDowell,
a division superintendent on the C. & S. C.,
and other less important employees of the
same road came in on every train. All over
the city was the exciting premonition that
something was going to happen. The army,
as Katherine had called it, was reënforced by
two fresh detachments brought in on the C. &
S. C. from no one knew just where, but they
were carefully guarded from being too much
in evidence, and there was not the least disorder. When noon came and nothing had
happened the tension relaxed a little, and the
town returned to its accustomed quiet.

At the M. & T. station, however, the excitement increased, manifesting itself in many ways.
The trains came in and went out on their sched-
uled time, and the routine work went on without
variation, but there was a nervous alertness evident everywhere. Train crews stood in little
knots about the platform and yards, speculating

about the fight whose issue meant much to each of them, but in which they had not as yet been able to take a part. At one forty-five No. 14, which leaves Truesdale at two o'clock for Tillman City, St. Johns, and Manchester, backed down to the station to take on its passengers. Carse, the conductor, stood near the cab talking to the engineer and the fireman, keeping all the while an eye on the passengers.

"We're getting a big crowd to-day," he observed. "That's McDowell of the C. & S. C. getting in the rear coach there. He's a mean brute. Ain't you glad we ain't under him, Downs?"

The engineer nodded emphatically, and climbing down from the cab, stood beside the conductor. "Seems to me," he said, "there are a lot of C. & S. C. boys taking this train. I've spotted three or four already."

"Say," exclaimed Carse, "do you suppose they're going back to Manchester to have another shot at the old man? I brought them back from there yesterday on No. 5, and they were the sickest crowd you ever saw. The old man can give them just about all they want."

He paused and glanced at his watch. "We

pull out in thirty seconds," he said. And at two o'clock No. 14 started northward on what was to prove a most eventful run in the history of the M. & T. The train rattled over the yard switches, slid creaking under the brakes down to the river, rumbled across the bridge, and then toiled up the first of the long grades between Truesdale and Sawyerville.

Carse was collecting tickets in the second car when suddenly it thrilled and trembled, and the train, with grinding squealing brakes, came to a stop. The conductor was all but thrown from his feet, but he staggered to the platform, and leaping down ran toward the engine, followed by an excited crowd of passengers.

"What's the matter?" he demanded of Downs, whom he found clambering out of the cab.

"That's what I want to know," answered the engineer. "Didn't you pull the signal cord?"

"No," said Carse, looking puzzled. "I wonder what's up."

At that moment a man came forward from the group of passengers: it was McDowell. "I signalled you to stop," he said.

Carse waited an instant for him to go on,

and then asked impatiently, "Well, what's wrong?"

"Nothing that I know of," said McDowell, easily. "I wanted the train to stop."

Carse stepped toward him angrily. "I don't know whether you're drunk or not," he said, "but that's a damned poor kind of a joke. You'll find that out as soon as we get to Sawyerville."

"Oh, no, I won't," said McDowell. "I'm superintendent of this road, and the first thing I'm going to do is to fire you. Haven," — he called to one of the group behind him, — "you can take this train to Manchester."

Another man pushed into the circle. He was Stewart, the sheriff of Evelyn County. "Mr. McDowell is quite right. Mr. Frederick McNally, the receiver of the road, appointed him this morning. And I now serve on you a writ from Judge Black —"

"See here," interrupted Carse, "are you sheriff of Evelyn County or of the whole United States? You'd better keep out of this; the county line's about half a mile back."

"We're wasting time," said McDowell, shortly. "James and Mangan, take the en-

N

gine.   We'll take charge of this train, sir,
county or no county."

"Not if I can help it," said Carse, under his
breath.   Then shouting, "Get away, boys;
don't mind me," he sprang upon McDowell,
hitting out swift and hard, and in a second the
two men were clinched and rolling in the sand.
Downs took the hint and, leaping into the cab,
let off the air brake and seized the throttle,
while Berg, his big fireman, wrenched free from
the two men who tried to hold him and rushed
toward the cab.   For a moment it looked as
though No. 14 was going to get away.

But the first detachment of Mr. McNally's
army was not at hand for nothing.   Berg was
pulled down from the step he had succeeded
in reaching, and a blow from behind stretched
him unconscious beside the track.   Downs
caught up the shovel which lay at his feet,
and brought it down hard on a man who was
climbing over the tender ; then without turning
he drove the handle squarely into the face of
another who was standing on the step and
trying to clutch his legs.   But the odds were
too great, and in a moment he was rushed back
against the fire-box, and his arms were pinioned

fast. McDowell had been freed from his assail-
ant by two of his brawny supporters, and he
rose to his feet with some difficulty; the blood
was streaming down his face, but he was quite
cool. Seeing that resistance was at an end, he
called to the men in the engine:—

"Let up on that man; we don't want to kill
him. Bring him down here."

A moment later, he said: "Put bracelets on
all three of them and take them into the smoker.
Some of you stay around and see that they don't
do any more mischief." Then turning to the
men he had already ordered to take charge of
the train, he said: "All right, boys, let her go.
We're nearly ten minutes late."

McNally's plans were well laid; so well laid
that McDowell's mistake in not stopping the
train soon enough did not prevent their being
carried out successfully. The sheriff of Malden
County had been told what was expected of him,
and he was waiting on the platform of the
Sawyerville station when No. 14 pulled in.
There had been no warning, there was no
possibility of resistance, and everything moved
as smoothly as clockwork. The writs were
served, the telegraph office seized, and the

M. & T. employees about the station replaced
by McDowell's "boys" almost before the dazed
incumbents knew what was happening. The
new telegraph operator wired to McNally, who
had already taken possession of the Truesdale
terminal, telling him briefly of the fight for the
train and the capture of Sawyerville. McNally
sent back brief instructions for the conduct of
the rest of the raid. They were told to make
no attempt to keep schedule time, but to go
slowly and cautiously, and to use as little violence as possible. Altogether McDowell had
reason to feel well satisfied when he came out
on the station platform ready to take his train
on its unique journey up the road.

There stood near him a number of passengers
gathered in an excited group, discussing the
fight, the delay of the train, and the somewhat
remote chance of getting to Manchester. One
of them, a very stout man with deep-set, watery
eyes and a florid complexion, recognized the
Superintendent and turned to him.

"Are we likely to have to wait as long as
this at every station?" he asked.

"I guess so," answered McDowell, shortly.

"This is an outrage," exclaimed the other,

angrily. "I took this train for the purpose of getting to Manchester."

"You'd better get aboard then," said Mc-Dowell. "We're going to start now."

His coolness exasperated the stout man, and he shouted after the Superintendent, "I won't submit to this. I tell you, you'll be sorry for it before I get through with you."

McDowell paid no heed to the threat, and nodded Haven to go ahead; but a young telegraph operator, whose services were to be required further up the road, heard the words and shouted to the angry man :—

"If you don't want to take the train, there's probably a livery stable here, or else you can go to the hotel. It's a gold cure, but I guess they'd take you in."

McDowell laughed and went into the car. He did not hear what his former passenger answered, and he did not care. He would probably have been less amused if he had known that the man was none other than State Senator "Sporty" Jones. It does not pay to enrage any man wantonly, and especially not a man who makes it his main principle in life to get even. And as any of his circumspect asso-

ciates could inform you, Senator Sporty Jones
was just such a man.

It was nearing six o'clock when No. 14
slowed down in the southern outskirts of Tillman City. The army, though depleted, was
jubilant, and more than made up in *esprit du
corps* what it had lost in numbers. The raid
had so far been completely successful: all the
stations had been seized, and the south-bound
trains they had met had been held up and
placed in charge of C. & S. C. employees.
There had been no resistance worth mention-
ing, and they had prevented any warning of
their coming from going up the line ahead of
them. Tillman City was lying an unsuspect-
ing prey, though fairly in their clutches.

Bill Stevens, the agent at Tillman, knew that
something had gone wrong, for No. 14 was
later than usual, and had not been reported
from the last two stations; so when the drooping semaphore told him that she was in the
block, he went out on the platform to find out
what had happened. As the train came panting up to the station he saw two strange men
in the cab instead of Downs and Berg, and this
puzzled him more than ever.

The sheriff was the first man off the train; he walked straight up to the agent, and in two minutes the formalities were over. Stevens and his subordinates were discharged, and the ticket office and baggage room put in charge of the new employees with a celerity born of practice. A number of deputies under McDowell's orders scattered out to take possession of the round-house, the freight depot, and the yards.

Still standing on the platform in an excited crowd of raiders, former employees, and station loafers, was the agent. He was thinking fast, for he saw the importance of getting word to Manchester of what was happening along the line. The telegraph line was in the hands of the enemy, but a locomotive — It was worth a trial, anyway. There were three at Tillman: 33 that had just brought in No. 14, 7 on a siding waiting to take the train to Manchester, and 10, the regular yard engine. The two passenger engines were out of the question, for they were already well guarded, but the little switching locomotive lay at the northern end of the yard, and had not as yet been seized by the deputies. In the confusion, and aided by the gathering dusk of the early October evening, something might be done.

Glancing around, Stevens saw Murphy, the hostler, standing at his elbow.   Without turning toward him he spoke softly.

"Murphy," he said, "slip out of this crowd and follow me. I'm going to try to get away on 10. I want you to throw a switch for me."

The hostler nodded without a word, and threaded his way after the agent to the edge of the platform.   Once out of the glare of the station lights there was less need for caution, and the two men set out at a rapid walk toward the north end of the yards.

Suddenly a deputy came out from behind a freight car and laid a detaining hand on the agent's arm.

"What are you up to?" he demanded.

There was no word of reply, but Murphy's fist shot out, landing dully on the man's jaw, and without an outcry he sank inert on the sand.

The agent darted forward, keeping out of the heavy sand by bounding along the irregularly laid ties, and in a moment he was climbing into the cab of the switch engine.

"Thank God! there's steam and water," he thought, and throwing over the reversing lever he grasped the throttle and came backing rapidly down the siding.

It was too dark for the men at the station to see perfectly what had happened, but they saw enough to excite their suspicion, and No. 33, which had already uncoupled from the train, ran up the main track to investigate. James and Mangan and a couple of deputies were in the cab.

Murphy had already thrown the switch and was standing beside it, holding a coupling pin in his hand, awaiting developments. The two locomotives were running right at each other, and unless somebody changed his mind very promptly a collision was inevitable; but the agent was in such a frame of mind that a smash-up was rather to his liking than otherwise, and he pulled the throttle a little wider open. He would waste no steam whistling, but grasping the hand rail he swung out from the cab and waved his free arm.

"Look out!" he yelled, "I'm coming."

Furthermore it was obvious to the men in 33 that he meant to keep on coming, and as none of them had any wish to try conclusions, even with little No. 10, the big locomotive stopped short and went backing down the track, the deputies shouting to their comrades at the station for reënforcements.

No. 10 slowed down as she backed on to the main track, and as Murphy threw the switch she stopped and then moved forward. Stevens waited for Murphy, who left the switch open and climbed into the cab. Then with a clear track before her No. 10 went tearing down the long grade as fast as her dumpy little drivers would carry her.

Halfway to Byron is a milk shed with a short siding, and when they reached it Stevens shut down and stopped with a jerk.

"Get out," he said to Murphy, "and throw over that switch and put out the lamp."

As they started on again he said dryly, "When they strike that, it may teach 'em to go slow for the rest of the run."

It was just six-seventeen by the station clock when Mason, the operator at Byron, heard No. 10 coming in. He ran out on the platform, but Stevens waved him back.

"Get in there," he said as he dropped from the cab. "I want you to send a message quick."

CHAPTER XIV

A CAPTURE AT BRUSHINGHAM

ON the same Wednesday morning Jawn Donohue was oiling the old switch engine preparatory to making up a train of coal cars. Since his ride with the President, Jawn had been even more silent than before. His work had been done with the same gruff independence, and his fireman had received the usual quota of stern rebukes; in fact, Jawn was outwardly so like his old self that none suspected him of emotion, but Jawn knew how thin was the veneer. It is hard upon a man to lose ground in the great struggle. Conscious of his ability, proud in his experience, Jawn grew daily more bitter at the prospect before him, and more hostile to his superiors. For a few days after the ride he had hoped for some word; he had felt that such an appeal as the one he had made to Jim Weeks should be productive of some notice, if not of a definite result. But as the

week wore away, and no word came, his heart
sank.   Every day he rattled the dumpy little
engine about the division yards, chewing the
stem of his pipe, and hardening his heart
against the world.   He spent Sunday in his
room at the boarding-house, for he had no
family.   Monday and Tuesday passed in worse
than solitude, and when Wednesday morning
came, and with it a message from the division
superintendent, Jawn, in spite of his hopes, was
taken by surprise.   The message was addressed
to the agent, and was very brief : —

Send J. Donohue and fireman to Manchester at once.

Jawn and his fireman took 16 for Manchester.
Beyond a brief word Jawn had said nothing,
but his heart was disturbed.   He was sure that
it couldn't mean discharge, for they would not
call him north for that — a word and a check
would have settled it.   It was hardly likely
that one of the passenger engineers was to be
reduced in his favor; Jawn knew the inside
history of every man's connection with the
road, and he could see no reason for a change.
No, as he worked it over and over in his mind

during the three-hour ride, he began to suspect that there was special work to be done.

If Jawn had been present at the brief scene in Mattison's office that morning, or if there had been a friend at court to tell him of it, he would have been a happy man. For while Jim Weeks, aggressive as ever, was organizing his forces for the defence of the road (Jim foresaw what Porter's next move in the natural course of events would be), Mattison had turned to the division superintendent, and said: "Who can you put on the engine, if we have to come to rough work? The nerviest man we've got." And before the other could reply, Jim had turned from a conversation with Harvey to say: "Donohue's got to take out that train. He's on a switch engine at Tillman."

Jim was continually surprising his subordinates with his intimate knowledge of the details of management. Mattison had long been accustomed to his ways, but he gave Jim a glance of wonder before he repeated the order to the division chief. And so Jawn was called to Manchester as the nerviest man on the road.

In the meantime a scene not unlike that at Truesdale was being enacted in and about the

Manchester station. There was the same reticence, and the studied quiet and perfect discipline were even more pronounced; for with Jim and Harvey to issue orders, and with Mattison and Mallory to execute them, the chance of a slip or a misunderstanding was too slight to be considered. A long train of tourist cars was made up shortly after noon and backed into the train shed, where it lay awaiting orders. Jim had no very definite idea of using it, at least until force was the only expedient; but he had been through too many fights to be caught off his guard. Instructions were wired from the despatcher's office to the operators all along the line, ordering them to report promptly any irregularity or suspicious circumstance. Meanwhile the regular trains for Truesdale pulled out through the yards and went on their way.

When Jawn came into the Superintendent's office at two o'clock he found a group of men standing in nervous attitudes, all evidently awaiting orders. A boy stopped him and asked his business.

"I want to see Mr. Mattison," said Jawn, removing his pipe and holding it awkwardly: Jawn, though at home on an engine, was ill at ease in an office.

" Can't see him," snapped the boy; " he's busy."

" He sent for me."

" Name, please."

" Donohue."

" Sit down, Mr. Donohue."

Jawn sat down in a corner and the boy disappeared. In a short time he returned and led Jawn to Mattison's desk. Mattison wasted no time, but told him the situation in a few sentences. " Now, Donohue," he said, in conclusion, " you understand, do you, that we are putting a big responsibility on you? Mr. West will be in command, and you will be subject to his orders without question; but if for any reason you should have to act rapidly, or should be thrown on the defensive, I shall expect you to do what is best for the road. Run no unnecessary risks, but remember, we must hold the line at any cost — if we lose an engine doing it. Do you understand? "

Jawn, standing beside the oak desk, looked down at the Superintendent and nodded gravely. Mattison returned the look with a brief searching gaze, then he turned to his work, saying, " Very well, you may go."

Harvey was all over the station. The strain of the last two days had told upon his nerves, but the prospect of a conflict buoyed him up. He had a long talk with Mallory, in which a campaign was mapped out as fully as was possible in the circumstances. It had been decided to hold the men ready to board the train at a moment's notice; but Harvey, as three o'clock came, ordered them aboard, for he realized that the longer the delay the greater would be the need of prompt action. So the long line filed out across the platform to the waiting cars, and the men made themselves comfortable for a long wait. Mallory stationed two of his own men in each car with orders to maintain strict discipline. In the baggage car were stored extra chains, hawsers, coupling links, crowbars, patent frogs, and every other device which, in Mattison's estimation, could be used in case of extreme circumstances, and there were chairs for Harvey and his lieutenants.

Later Harvey walked up to the engine, where Jawn and his fireman were oiling and polishing.

"Everything all right, Donohue?" he asked.

Jawn growled and looked back at the coal in the tender.

"She ain't much of an engine," he replied.

Harvey looked her over. She was an ordinary light yard engine with a footboard in place of the pilot and with a sloping tank. He called to the yard master who stood near.

"Haven't you got a better engine than this, Pratt?"

Pratt came across the platform.

"I understood you wanted an old one," he said.

"We do," replied Harvey; "but we want one that will hold a little water, and one that can make time if necessary."

"Shall I change, sir?"

"It rests with the engineer. Donohue, can you do anything with this engine?"

Jawn leaned against the cab and slowly shook his head.

"Get another, then," said Harvey, and as the change was effected Jawn's heart was won. In an unreasoning way he promptly attributed his changed condition to Harvey; for in spite of his gruff shell the kernel of Jawn's nature was keenly susceptible to kindness, and to him a good engine and plenty of authority was the greatest kindness in life.

o

For two hours the train waited. Then, at five o'clock, a detail was sent into the restaurant, and the men were supplied with sandwiches and coffee, eating without leaving their seats. In half an hour all were fed, and they stretched out on the cane seats as comfortably as their crowded condition permitted. The long wait did not improve tempers, and it was a sullen, weary train load that counted the minutes on into the dusk. Jawn sat on his high seat and dozed.

The suspense was even more tense in the offices on the second floor of the station. Jim and Harvey spent most of the time in the private office, going over every possible combination of circumstances, Jim giving Harvey explicit directions for each case—when to use force, when not, when to call on the law, and when to send for aid. Occasionally Jim would call in Mattison to ask a question concerning some detail of the road, or he would send for Mallory to explain more fully his directions. It was plain that Jim desired to leave nothing to chance, now that the real struggle was on, but to throw all his available resources into the conflict. Mattison had a map drawn for Harvey, which showed every station, curve, switch, and siding; this Harvey studied during the lulls in the conversation, and as he already was familiar with all but the minor details of construction, he soon had his information upon a working basis. At six-fifteen Mattison came in.

"Mr. Weeks," he said, "the despatcher reports something the matter. For two or three hours, he says, the local reports have been confused and unsatisfactory. A few minutes ago he called up Tillman City and hasn't yet succeeded in getting any reply. The local men are sending in train reports, but something isn't right. He's got a notion that they aren't our old men."

"Tell them to try again," said Jim. "Ask them something a new man wouldn't know."

Mattison left the office and hurried to the stairway. On the landing he met a newsboy who was running up, calling: —

"Shcago Even' Papers! Extry! All about big railroad war!"

Mattison seized a paper and glanced at the headings. "Fight for M. & T.," he read. "Trunk Line Gobbles Small Road." His eye ran over the article; it was dated that afternoon from Truesdale. He turned and ran up the stairs, dashing into Jim's office and spreading the paper on the table.

"It's up to us," he said. "They've been at work all the afternoon."

As he spoke a boy came running into the office.

"Message from Byron, sir."

Mattison snatched the paper and read aloud,—

C. & S. C. train leaving Tillman north seizing road.
                                        STEVENS.

"That's the Tillman agent," said Mattison. "What's he doing at Byron?"

"Probably had to run for it," responded Harvey, putting on his hat and buttoning his coat. "That means fast work. Clear the track for me, Mattison."

"Wait a minute," said Jim. "Have we any trains north of Byron?"

"No."

"Then don't send any orders. They would warn the other side. No, go ahead and beat them if you have to break their heads."

As Harvey dashed out of the office Jim's eyes sparkled. He liked to do his own fighting, and

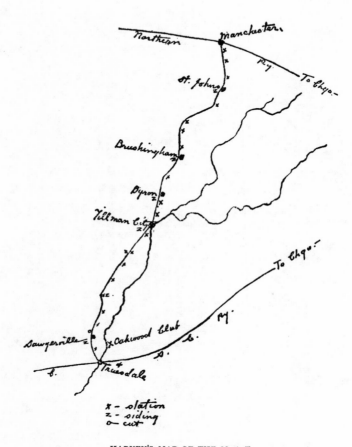

x — station
z — siding
o — cut

HARVEY'S MAP OF THE M. & T.

it was half regretfully that he turned to the Superintendent.

"If they're as near as that, Mattison, it means trouble. You'd better collect another gang and send it out after West. Take men off the trains, out of the yards, anywhere you can get them."

The wheels were soon in motion again, and another train backed under the iron roof and slowly filled with brawny men.

Harvey swung aboard his train and it started with a jerk, rolling rapidly over the network of tracks, past the switch tower, under the signal bridge, and out toward the open country. The little army was not sullen now. Figures sat erect, eyes flashed, young men spoke eagerly, older ones gruffly, and through the train ran a steady murmur of inquisitive wonder. Apparently, save for a few dozen sticks and clubs, the men were not armed, but many hip pockets bulged suspiciously.

In the baggage car Harvey and Mallory were talking earnestly. Mallory was for travelling slowly lest they should encounter a loose rail or an open switch, but Harvey disagreed. He spread the map out on a box and rested a finger on the dot marked Tillman City.

"There they are," he said, "or were a few

minutes ago, and they're coming right toward us. Now, to keep us from getting word they have to stop at every telegraph station, and that takes time. We've got a clear track and can travel fully twice as fast as they can. Here" — he moved his finger up the line of the road — "here at Brushingham is a long siding. I want to make that siding before they do."

"Why?"

"Because we must pass them there."

"They aren't going to lie up and let us run by."

"Yes, they are," said Harvey. "Wait a moment." He called to a brakeman who stood at the door, "Go up to the engine and tell the engineer to get to the siding at Brushingham at full speed."

The man nodded and ran forward. Another moment and those in the baggage car felt a jerk and a lift, and soon they were rattling over the rails with sway and roll. Harvey, meantime, was explaining to Mallory a plan which made that veteran chuckle merrily. His eyes wandered to the heap of chains, ropes, and iron piled on each side of the rear door, and he chuckled again. But Harvey's face was serious.

"It's something of a question whether we can get there in time, Mallory. It's a sixty-five mile run for us to thirty-eight for them. We have all the advantage, of course, but there won't be any time to spare." He drew out his watch and timed the clicks of the rails. "He's hitting it up in good style."

"What are we making?"

"About fifty, and pulling up all the time. It won't take us much over an hour at this rate, and I don't believe that they can make it in anything like that time. There are a lot of little stations north of Tillman, and they've got to stop at every one."

Nevertheless, as the minute hand crept around the watch, the two men began to peer out through the side window. It was dark now, and as the landmarks were not too familiar either to Harvey or to Mallory, they were unable to get their bearings.

"Where are we?" Harvey called to the brakeman.

"Getting into St. Johns," was the reply.

Sure enough, in another moment colored yard lights were whizzing by. There was a great clatter as they took the switches, then a row of streaked electric lights, a dim impression of streets and of clanging bells, a shriek from the locomotive, and again they were in the open. A few minutes later Harvey gave orders that a brakeman climb forward on the engine ready to throw the Brushingham switch. Soon the car jarred and struggled under the air brake, and then slowed down, grinding and pounding, almost to a stop. The brakes were released, and the train rolled easily out beyond the station on to the long siding. Harvey pulled the signal cord.

"Now, Mallory," he said, as the train came to a standstill, "we can go ahead."

Mallory picked up a patent frog from the floor, and with Harvey and the brakeman swung out of the car and ran down the track. From the windows projected a long row of heads, but no questions were asked as the three men ran forward. A short distance ahead of the engine they stopped. Away to the south a small bright light rounded into view.

"Here she comes," said Mallory.

Harvey made no reply, and the frog was adjusted to the east rail of the main track. Then they went back and clambered aboard the engine. Mallory ordered a squad of men forward, and stationed some on the pilot and running board, others on the tender and front platform. The light grew slowly larger, sending out pointed rays and throwing a shine on the rails. There was the sound of a bell and of the exhaust, and the train pulled slowly toward the bleak little station. Suddenly, when within speaking distance, the approaching engine struck the patent frog and left the rails with a jar and a scrape, ploughing her nose into the slag.

"Go ahead," said Harvey.

Jawn pulled the throttle lever, and the long train moved slowly southward. No. 14 was not full now. The process of dropping men at every station had left only about half the employees, who clustered in the forward cars and looked curiously at the passing train. At a shouted order from Mallory, one of his men dropped off with a squad at his back and took possession of the wreck, while Harvey, flushed with victory, moved on to undo the work of the afternoon.

CHAPTER XV

DEUS EX MACHINA

As Senator Sporty Jones stood on the Saw-yerville platform and watched No. 14 vanishing round a curve, his rage against the Superintendent cooled somewhat and hardened into a determination to make somebody pay. The more he thought of it the clearer it grew that the "somebody" should be a bigger man than McDowell, though Sporty meant to get even with him, too, some day. He knew, as did every one who had read the newspapers, the broad outlines of the fight between Weeks and Porter for the road. As he thought it over, the problem seemed to grow more complicated. The Senator hated the two men about equally and had a long score against each of them; for though both were lobbyists on a large scale, neither of them had thought him worth conciliating. He was afraid lest in trying to hurt one he might help the other.

He was capable of quick, clear thinking, and as he ran over in his mind what he knew of the fight, he saw that what encouraged these men so openly to resort to violence was a judicial deadlock. There was just one force which could profitably be appealed to now, the State Executive.

He walked slowly down the rickety wooden steps and across the road; then, after looking about irresolutely, he turned toward the weather-beaten little hotel.

Before he had gone far the deposed station agent overtook him. He was smoking a cigarette with short, nervous puffs, and he fell in step with the Senator, evidently relieved at having a chance to talk.

"What did you think of that?" he asked. "Pretty sudden, wasn't it?"

The Senator grunted a savage assent, and the agent went on : —

"Well, all I say is, these fellows needn't think they've got any cinch until Jim Weeks has had his innings. He's going to have it, too. This kind of a scrap is right in his line."

The Senator seemed to be listening, and the agent was encouraged to try his hand at

prophesying what would happen when Jim
Weeks should come down the line. When they
reached the hotel both men paused, and the
Senator said affably, —

"Come in and have something."

"All right, if you mean ginger ale," laughed
the agent. "It's a temperance house, with a
gold cure on the side."

The disgust of Senator Sporty Jones was
expressed with such blasphemous force that the
agent was moved to add, —

"You can get anything you want down in the
next block."

"All right," grunted the Senator. "Wait a
minute, though; I want to telephone."

"There ain't a telephone in town," said the
agent. "The line goes up the other side of the
river to Tillman. I don't believe you can find a
'phone nearer than Truesdale."

"How far's that?" asked the Senator, after
an expressive pause.

"'Bout fifteen miles by the river road. You
have to go round by way of Oakwood. It's
going to rain, too," he added, glancing at the
clouded sky.

The look of annoyance on the Senator's face

settled into one of determination, and the agent began to fear lest the invitation to "have something" had slipped from the great man's mind.

The Senator asked slowly, "Is there such a thing as a livery stable in this" — he gulped — "in this town?"

"I guess old man Barnes could let you have some sort of a horse. He's got a place just the other side of Hogan's. I'll go down there with you if you like."

The parley with Barnes took only a few minutes, and at half-past three the Senator drove down the main street and turned west toward the river road. His vehicle was a light delivery wagon with a canopy over it, and was drawn by a ragged old white horse, which, according to the livery man, was an exceptional animal.

"The General's an aristocrat, he is," said Barnes. "I might say a thoroughbred. I hate like poison to let him out to a stranger, but I let you take him because I see you understand a horse."

There was no flicker of intelligence in the agent's face as he heard the words, but when the Senator asked him to accompany him on the drive he declined. " I want to be on hand," he explained, "when Jim Weeks comes down the line." So Senator Jones started out alone on his drive to Truesdale, and the agent watched him from the door of Hogan's saloon. "Go along with him!" he thought. "I guess not. It'd be a circus, though, to see what happens when they get to the river bridge." Then, as Barnes joined him on the steps, he added, "What do you suppose the General will do to him?"

"Oh, he won't hurt him," answered Barnes. "He'll just turn around and come home when he gets good and ready. Come in and have something."

The General took a violent dislike to the Senator. It annoyed him to have people try to make him go whither he would not, and he shook his head angrily in response to the impatient jerks at the reins. When the Senator tried to accelerate the pace by whacking his toughened flanks with the whip, he kicked up his heels derisively and then stumbled along more wearily if possible than before.

The miles crept by as slowly as he could wish, and he was pleased when they passed a fork of the road and he knew he was being

driven to the river. He disliked rivers, and
had long ago decided that he would never cross
one. That his resolution had once been broken
was not his fault, for they had dragged him
over the Oakwood bridge at the end of a stout
rope; but this only made him firmer in his
determination, and people who drove him were
wont to stay on the west side of the river.

Old man Barnes had given the Senator no
hint of this prejudice of the aristocratic animal
he was driving, so he had no foreboding of
what was going to happen. Now that he had
made up his mind that it was worse than use-
less to try to interfere with the General, he was
jogging along in comparative comfort, regardless of the rain which had grown from a fine
drizzle to a steady downpour. He thought the
chances were in favor of his reaching Truesdale and a telephone by midnight. He smiled
at the thought, for he had evolved a scheme
that would disconcert both of the contestants
for the M. & T. alike, and would show them
that he, State Senator Sporty Jones, was not a
man to be sneezed at.

About a half a mile above the Oakwood Club
House and in full view of it the road crosses the

river, and the Senator noticed the big, rambling building on top of the hill, and wondered if they had a telephone there. " I'll try and see, anyway," he thought.

The General turned willingly up the approach to the bridge, increasing his speed to an almost respectable trot. When he reached the top he stopped in his tracks and stared with disfavor at the worn planks before him. The Senator snatched the whip from its socket and beat upon the General until his arms were tired. At every blow the horse would kick feebly, and then resume a droop-eared attitude, as though grieving over the depravity of man. The Senator looked around helplessly, but there was no aid in sight, so he climbed down from the wagon and walked around to the bridle. The General may have suspected another attempt at dragging, for a vicious snap of his yellow teeth caused the Senator to step back out of reach, completely baffled. He stared an instant at the solemn face before him and then shaking the whip he said, —

"You've got me down this time, damn you, but I'll — "

The Senator stopped, his favorite threat

unuttered, threw the whip into the river and turning, walked slowly across the bridge, and as he went the story he meant to tell over the 'phone to the Governor grew to fearful proportions. As for the General, when he saw that the victory was won, he turned about and sauntered back to Sawyerville.

In the party of golfers whom the rain had driven from the links to the shelter of the Oakwood Club was Katherine. She had gone once around the short course and perversely enough her score was unusually good; but she could not get her mind off the more exciting game which she knew must be in progress along the railway line west of the river. Altogether she welcomed the rain, and was glad when its increasing violence drove them to the shelter of the club house. There at least she was near a telephone. She had no disposition to make one of the merry group of men and girls who were drying out before the crackling log fire, but after a moment of hesitation she joined the circle.

One of the men was standing by a window, peering through a field-glass at the more ardent

P

and impervious enthusiasts who were still following the ball.

" The rain's letting up a bit," he said at length.
"You can really see things — hello ! "

The group before the fire turned toward him,
attracted by the long silence which followed the
exclamation. They saw a look of puzzlement
on his face which gradually gave place to a
broad grin.

"What's up ? " asked somebody.

" By George," he exclaimed, lowering the
glass, "that's funny." He raised the glass
again and this time his shoulders shook.

" I didn't know anybody out on the links
could be as funny as that," one of the girls
observed.

" He isn't on the links," answered the man
with the glass, " he's on the bridge. And the
horse is turning round and going back." With
which singularly lucid preface, the young man
told what he had seen of the General's victory
at the Oakwood bridge.

It was about fifteen minutes later when Sporty
appeared, dripping and mud bespattered, but
kept warm by glowing fires of indignation,
and vigorously demanded of the attendant the

use of the telephone. At the sound of his voice one of the older men turned quickly and approached him with a word of greeting. "But what's the matter with you, man?" he added, noting the Senator's sorry condition.

"They're having a riot on the railroad," answered Sporty. "Can I use your 'phone?"

"Sure," answered the other. "Right this way," and the two men crossed the hall and disappeared in the office. A few minutes later the man came back and rejoined the group.

"He's State Senator Jones, Sporty Jones, you know. He says they're having no end of a time over on the railroad. When I left him he seemed to be trying to telephone all over the State at once."

"I've heard of him," said Katherine, "but I've never met him. I wish you'd bring him here after he gets through telephoning." And the man with some surprise said he would.

The Senator did not reappear from the office for nearly an hour, and in that time he worked fast. He began by calling up Representative Jim Cleary of the Seventh District, a man with influence who happened to be in the capital on business. The Senator wasted no oratory on

him, he simply told him what it was necessary
to do.   After that he talked with other men
about the State, and repeated what he had said
to Jim Cleary, suggesting to them the proper
way for putting "pressure" on the Governor.
Then, having prepared his avalanche, he telephoned to the executive mansion and asked for
the Governor.   He learned from the Secretary
that the Governor was busy, but would be at
liberty in a few minutes.

"All right," said Sporty.   "Let me know
when he's ready to talk to me."

He rang off and rose from his chair, stiffly,
for the damp and the cold had struck through.
The man he knew appeared at his elbow, and
leading him in to the fire introduced him to those
who were still grouped about it, to Katherine
last of all.

"You must have had an afternoon full of
experiences," she said.

"Yes," answered the Senator.   "I enjoyed
my drive over from Sawyerville immensely.
The weather was somewhat unpleasant, but I
had an excellent horse and we made very good
time, until we got a hot-box.   I was obliged to
leave the vehicle with a farmer, and walked the
last two miles."

"Indeed?" said Katherine. "But please tell me about the riot. It must have been very exciting."

"I hardly think it would interest a lady," said Sporty, uneasily.

"Senator Jones," — Katherine was speaking with much severity, — "I did not think when I first saw you that you could prove so disagreeable."

Sporty beamed. "It wasn't very much of a riot," he said. "They just hit the fireman behind the ear and put handcuffs on the engineer, and started out to grab the road. They'll have to fight for it."

"Was what they did legal?" she asked.

"Oh, no; not at all. It's just a hold-up."

The Senator was saying rather more than he meant to, and he was glad that the telephone bell broke off the conversation at this point. He excused himself abruptly and went to have a talk with the Governor.

Katherine walked to a window and stood staring out with unseeing eyes. At last she turned to a man who stood near her and said : —

"I don't believe it's going to rain any more. Will you have them bring up my trap, please?"

CHAPTER XVI

McNALLY'S EXPEDIENT

KATHERINE'S casual acquaintances thought of
her as a cool, unemotional young woman, and
when asked for their estimate of her would give
it with confidence that it was accurate. The
few who knew her better were less sure what
they thought of her, and there was considerable
diversity in their opinions. She had a strong
will and plenty of confidence in it. Until she
had found herself standing between Harvey
West and her father, she never had the least
doubt that in any situation she would be able to
do what she wanted. But without knowing it
she liked to let her impulses direct her, and her
confidence that her will could, if necessary,
overrule them gave them freer play than they
would have had in a weaker personality. She
was keenly sensitive — and this she recognized
— to the atmosphere of her immediate envi-
ronment.

To-day the gray of the dripping sky and the sullen river and the pasty macadam road seemed to have got into her thoughts and to pervade everything. There was a feeling of eternity in the gathering twilight as though there had never been anything else and never would be. But she knew there had; it was only three days since she and Harvey had driven along this road. She recalled the glisten of the sunlight on the river, and the crimson of the hard maples stained by the first early frost, and she knew it was not the sunshine nor the tingle in the air nor the beautiful way in which Ned and Nick flew along stride for stride over the hard white road, but something else, something quite different, which had made her glad that Sunday morning. She looked straight ahead and tried to imagine that not the wooden English groom, but Harvey, sat beside her. Then realizing whither her imaginings were drifting, she pulled herself up sharply. "You sentimental idiot!" she thought.

The groom spoke. "Beg pardon, Miss Katherine?" and she knew she must have thought aloud.

Just then a black tree stump at the roadside

seemed to spring out of the ghostly twilight, and Nick, who never had the blues, amused himself by shying at it. Ned caught the spirit of the lark and over the next mile these two good friends of Katherine's supplied her with just the kind of tonic she needed.

It was late when she reached home and she had but a narrow margin of time left in which to dress for dinner; but telling the groom not to take the horses to the stable she hurried into the house and came out a moment later with a handful of sugar. The two beautiful heads turned toward her as she came down the steps and Nick gave a satisfied little whicker. She fed them alternately, a lump at a time, talking to them all the while in the friendly bantering way they liked. She was quite impartial with the sugar, but while Ned with lowered head was sniffing at her pockets for more, she laid her cheek against Nick's white, silky nose and whispered to him: —

"I think I like you best to-night. You did just right to shy at that stump. No, Ned, it wouldn't be good for you to eat any more sugar just before dinner. Good-by. If it wouldn't shock father and dent the floor, I'd take you into the house with me. But I don't suppose you'd like it, though."

Katherine was glad she was late and that she had to dress in a hurry. What she dreaded was being left alone with nothing to do but think. She had gone over the ground again and again until she had lost her sense of proportion. She had tried to believe that the raid was right and that her father's methods were above reproach; she had tried to be unwavering in her loyalty to his cause, but in spite of herself McNally's allusions and the fragmentary conversations she had overheard raised doubts which her father's evasions did not set at rest. In spite of herself her sympathies swung to the square, straightforward, courageous young fellow who had got into her heart without her knowing it. She had tried to make herself believe her father's insinuations about Jim Weeks; but what Harvey had told her, in his undiscriminating, hero-worshipping way, had made too deep an impression for that.

When she had finished dressing, as she stood before the mirror to take a final survey, she addressed a parting remark to the figure in the glass : —

" It won't do you any good to go on bothering this way. You haven't anything to do now
but go down to dinner and be as charming as
possible, particularly to Mr. McNally, whom
you cordially detest. When the time comes to
do something, I hope you'll do it right."

It was just seven o'clock when she came down
the stairs to be informed by the butler that the
gentlemen had not come home yet, and should
he serve dinner at once?

Katherine waited nearly half an hour, trying
to amuse herself with a very pictorial magazine,
and, finding that tiresome, by playing coon songs
at the piano. But the piano reminded her of Mr.
McNally, and she didn't want to think of him;
so giving up trying to wait she ordered dinner.

Dining alone when you have made up your
mind to it beforehand is not an unmixed evil;
but in Katherine's frame of mind it was about
as irritating as anything could be. When it
was over she called for her coffee in a big cup,
and she drank it, black and bitter, with a relish.
The frown which for the last hour had been
contracting her level brows disappeared, for
she had thought of something to do. As she
rose from the table she said to the butler : —

"Will you order the carriage, please, right away. I'm going out."

Porter was with McNally in one of the offices of the M. & T. station. The two had been sitting there ever since the building had been seized by the deputies, getting satisfactory reports from station after station as the raiders moved up the line. Porter was on the point of starting home for dinner when the reports began coming in from Tillman City. The first of the yellow sheets the boy brought them simply repeated the news that had come in so many times that afternoon. The station was in the hands of the C. & S. C. men, and there had been no resistance. But the second sheet was less satisfactory, for it told of Stevens's escape on the yard engine.

Porter read it and exclaimed petulantly, "McDowell must have been asleep when he let a man get away like that."

"Do you think there's much harm done?" asked McNally.

"I'm afraid so. Weeks will hear all about it in a few minutes, if he hasn't already, and he's sure to hit back. He moves quick, too."

"We can wire McDowell to stay right where

he is, and rush through another train with re-
enforcements," suggested McNally. "We may
not be able to get the rest, but we can at least
keep what we've got."

"You'd better make up another train, anyway. We can fill it up with men from our car-
shops. McDowell had better keep right on up
the line. If we have to fight, it'll be better
to do it at some small place than at Tillman.
We're less likely to be interfered with. Tell
McDowell to go slow and not too far."

The order to McDowell with the promise of
reënforcements was sent out in time to catch
him before he left Tillman, and then McNally
turned his attention to massing his reserve. At
the end of an hour and a half of hard work he
saw the last files of the rear guard march down
the platform and into the train. His frown expressed dissatisfaction, for these men were not
so good fighting material as those McDowell
had captained. Their manner was sheepish;
they did not finger lovingly the clubs they had
been provided with, and altogether they seemed
to feel a much greater respect for law and order
than was appropriate to the occasion.

They were the best men available, however,

and there were several hundred of them, and
McNally was about to give the order which
would send them up the road to the succor of
McDowell, when Porter came hurrying toward
him from the telegraph office.

"Don't send those men out yet, McNally,"
he said. "There's something wrong here. I
think they've bagged McDowell."

The train despatcher came into the waiting
room, and seeing them walked rapidly toward
them.

"Something has gone wrong, gentlemen.
We've been talking to Gilsonville and he's all
balled up. He isn't the same man who was
there fifteen minutes ago."

"They've got past McDowell then," said
McNally. "And they couldn't have done that
without catching him. We'd better get that train
away as fast as possible then, hadn't we?"

"I don't think so," said Porter. "Have
them ready to start at a minute's notice, and
we'll plan out what's the best thing to do."

Back in the little office again Porter explained his plan. "You see," he said, "these
fellows are not likely to be very much in a
fight. We don't know how many men Weeks

has got, but the farther down the line he comes the weaker he'll be. If we let him come far enough we can do the same trick to him that he must have done to McDowell; but if we meet him halfway, he may beat us. That leaves us at his mercy."

"Do you think Weeks is on the train himself?" asked McNally.

"Can't tell. It would be like him. If he isn't, that young West is. Most likely West is, anyway."

"He's the man that blocks our game, if he is a fool. If anything should happen to him, there wouldn't be any question as to who was receiver of the road."

Porter said nothing and there was a long silence. Then McNally went on, speaking slowly and guardedly: —

"If there is anything of a mix-up such a thing would be likely enough to happen. He's young enough and cocky enough to get hurt quite naturally."

Then Porter spoke quickly, for he read the unsaid meaning in the words. "That's going too far. I want the road, but not that way."

McNally's drooping lids quivered, but other-

wise his face was expressionless. He made no
pretence that Porter had misunderstood him.
He spoke as though unheeding the interrup-
tion.

"If we bring about his disappearance for a
day or two,—it needn't hurt him any,—we'll
control the road, fight or no fight."

He had meant to say something more, but
he stopped, his eyes fixed on the opening door.
Following his gaze Porter turned.

"Katherine!" he exclaimed.

With automatic courtesy, McNally rose and
drew up a chair for her, but Katherine did not
take it. She had worn a high-collared black
velvet cloak over her house dress, and she drew
it off and threw it over the desk. Then coming
up behind her father she touched his forehead
lightly with her cool hands.

"Keeping everlastingly at it," she said, trying to speak lightly, "without any dinner or
anything. Is business getting so very, very
serious?"

The tenderness of it touched Porter, and
though he felt that she should not be there he
could not send her away.

"We're right in the thick of it now," he said.

"It will all be over one way or the other in a day or two."

"And then," said Katherine, with a little laugh, "and then I'll have somebody to play with again."

She stooped and kissed him, and then noticing that McNally was still standing she addressed him for the first time.

"Please don't wait for me to sit down. I'm going to stay right here."

Porter yielded to the restfulness of having her there and sat with closed eyes, while she stroked the trembling lids with the tips of her fingers. Neither of the men spoke, and at last Katherine broke the silence.

"Don't you think," she said to her father, "that everything would go just as well if you came home with me now and took a little rest? You'll feel lots better to-morrow, if you do, and there's a to-morrow coming, you know. It isn't likely that anything more will happen to-night, is it?"

"I'm afraid it is," said McNally. "You see we think Weeks is coming down the line now, with a trainful of armed men, and he may force us into a fight before morning."

"I see," said Katherine. "That is, when his army meets the one you sent up the line this afternoon."

Porter moved his head free from her hands and asked sharply, —

"What do you know about that, dear?"

"Just what Senator Jones told me," she answered. "He got off the train at Sawyerville and drove over to the Club to telephone."

"Do you know which Senator Jones it was?" asked McNally. "Was it the one they call 'Sporty'?"

"Yes," laughed Katherine; "I'm very sure it was that one."

McNally turned quickly to Porter. "He's got it in for your people, hasn't he?"

"Yes," the other answered; "but he can't do much harm. Nobody pays any attention to him. Do you know, Katherine, whether his telephoning had anything to do with us?"

"I'll tell you everything I know about it," she said, and she recounted what she knew of the doings of the Senator on that afternoon.

"Is that bad news?" she asked, when she had finished.

Q

" We can hardly tell till we see what happens next," said McNally.

Katherine seated herself in the chair McNally had placed for her, and listened while her father and McNally talked over their plans and speculated upon the probable import of the messages which kept coming in. There was no attempt to keep Katherine in the dark as to what their plans were, and for the time she had given up looking at the perplexing aspects of the situation, and was enjoying the action and excitement of it. But as the clock ticked off one hour and then another, she noted her father's increasing weariness, and she determined to make another attempt to get him home, where he could, at least, have a few hours' rest.

She rose, and walking around behind him, as she had done before, she clasped her hands over his eyes, and said : —

" You're completely worn out, dad. Please come home. I don't believe anything is going to happen after all."

Porter sighed wearily ; but he said, " My dear, if Jim Weeks is coming down the line, something is sure to happen."

" Do you think he's on the train himself ? " she asked.

McNally looked up quickly. It was not the question, but something that the question suggested to him, that made him say : —

"Probably not. We think young West is in charge of the gang."

Katherine's hands were still clasped over her father's eyes, and McNally took the opportunity this afforded him to accompany his words with a meaning look that was insolent in its intentness. In spite of herself Katherine felt the blood mounting into her cheeks and forehead, and McNally, seeing the blush, made no effort to conceal his smile. Katherine did not flinch from his gaze, but returned it squarely. Dropping her hands to her father's shoulders, she said steadily : —

"I suppose he is on the train. He likes that sort of thing. Of course Mr. McNally will lead our forlorn hope when it starts out."

She smiled as she said it, for he winced under the thrust.

He rose hurriedly, and as he moved toward the door he spoke to Porter.

"I've got some business to attend to with Wilkins. I'll be back soon."

When he had left the room Porter turned to Katherine.

"You'd better go home now. I can't go until we know what is going on out on the road. I'll come as soon as I can, but you must go now."

He had spoken gently, but with a finality that left Katherine no hope of persuading him. He took up her cloak and threw it over her shoulders, and kissed her.

"Good night. I'll come along by and by."

"If you don't, I'll come back after you."

Without waiting to hear her father's dissent, which she knew would follow this declaration, she fled from the room and down the steps to her carriage.

As she settled herself among the robes and cushions she heard McNally's voice:—

"Can you find the right men to do it?"

The door slammed and the carriage clattered away with Katherine wondering what "it" was.

CHAPTER XVII

IN THE DARK

AFTER leaving Brushingham, Harvey and his crew merely duplicated the enemy's performance of the afternoon. The C. & S. C. employees were thrown out before they had become thoroughly settled, and with each new capture messages flew back to Mattison at Manchester, giving him and Jim Weeks a detailed account of the progress of the train. The greatest care was exercised to keep news of the train from Truesdale. Wherever there was a possibility of the ejected men reaching a telephone, they were actually taken in custody and placed under guard. The operators were instructed to answer all messages from the Truesdale despatcher as intelligently as possible, in order to continue the deception.

It was a long, hard ride. Harvey was called upon constantly to exercise ingenuity in the handling of his forces, and though Mallory was

of great assistance, the strain of responsibility
rested upon Harvey. He was tired when he
started, but as the night wore on toward morning, nothing but his sound nerves kept him
on his feet. At two-thirty o'clock they were
within twenty miles of Truesdale, and Harvey
and Mallory were both in the engine, anxiously looking for obstructions. From Mattison's despatches they knew that reënforcements
were flying down over an open road, but the
collecting of a second force had taken time, and
it was nearly midnight before the second train
was on its way, a hundred and sixty-five miles
from Harvey's present location.

Nearly all Harvey's men had been dropped
along the line, and he was in no position for
a conflict, particularly as he had no knowledge of the enemy's location or preparedness.
Mallory was for pausing until the other train
should reach them, probably about daylight.
He argued that they had nothing to gain
and everything to lose. Harvey, undecided,
referred to his map, spreading it out on the
fireman's bench while Mallory lighted matches
and held them over the paper. Harvey ran his
finger down the line to Sawyerville.

"Just north of the Sawyerville station," he said, "there is a curve and a deep cut. I am inclined to think that if they try to block the road they'll do it there. The quarries are right at hand, and all they need to do is to roll a few rocks down."

"Do you think they would try that?" asked Mallory. "It would block them worse than it would us."

"I don't know about that, but I'll feel a lot easier when we're through that cut with open country between us and Truesdale. Run slow, Donohue, and put out your headlight. Mallory, you see that the train is perfectly dark. We might as well try a little bluffing even if we do strike them. They won't know but what we've got five hundred men aboard, and the others will reach us before they find it out."

Mallory clambered over the coal in the tender, while the fireman crawled out on the running board and extinguished the headlight. The night was very dark, and Jawn leaned out of the cab window, his left hand gripping the throttle lever. The fireman was badly in need of sleep, and showed a tendency to grumble in a half-incoherent way, but Jawn was as silent

as at the start. To Harvey, who even in the
excitement was afraid to sit down for fear of
falling asleep, the engineer was a marvel in his
machine-like self-control.

Slowly the line of empty cars rolled along.
Jawn's eyes were glued to the track in front,
which to Harvey seemed a constantly resolving
confusion of shadows. The tall gray telegraph
poles crept by with monotonous regularity until
Harvey turned away and looked out at the dim
meadows on the left, over which was spread a
ghostly film of mist.

"There's the cut," said Jawn.

Harvey looked forward, but could see nothing. Jawn, however, gradually slackened speed
until they were barely moving. Mallory appeared on the tender and came over the coal
to the apron, where he stood leaning out with
one arm around the cab door-post. The fireman heaped a shovel with coal, and staggering
wearily into the cab he knocked open the door
of the fire-box from which a dull glow tem-
pered the darkness. Harvey seated himself on
the fireman's seat, holding himself stiffly erect
and trying to distinguish the track before.
Jawn slowly brought the train to a stop.

"What is it?" asked Harvey. "See anything ahead?"

"No. We're about two hundred yards from the curve."

Harvey turned to Mallory.

"We'd better throw out a few men ahead, Mallory, to see that the track is clear."

"Haven't got many left, not more than half a dozen altogether."

Harvey stepped down and stretched his tired limbs.

"I'll go myself," he said. "Call one of your men up here."

Mallory climbed back on the tender and whistled. A man who had been sitting on the steps of the first car came forward.

"You wait here, Donohue," said Harvey. "If everything is all right, I'll come back." He struck a match and looked at his watch. "We've been taking time enough. It's three-fifteen now. I'll walk along the top of the cut on the left-hand side, and you " — to the detective — "you take the other side. Keep within easy hail — " He paused abruptly. Through the crisp night air came the roll and snort of an engine. There was a long silence in the cab.

" She's running slow," said Jawn, at length.

Harvey stood breaking the match into bits. The noise of the other train came slowly nearer, but so slowly that all listened breathlessly. After a little they could hear the rumbling of an exhaust, and Jawn muttered, " She's stopped."

"We'd better wait," said Mallory. "It's more than likely that they have another gang ready for us. They probably will be coming this way before long."

Harvey stepped up to the fireman's seat again, and fixed his eyes on the black cut ahead. It was still dark, but he could now distinguish the deep shadow which marked the spot where the track bent sharply to the left between its rock walls. For some time all were silent, listening to the noise of the other engine. Jawn sat on his bench, which he had not left for hours, ready either for going ahead or for backing, as the circumstances should dictate. Mallory moved to the step and swung out as before, watching and listening. The fireman swung his arms and shifted his feet in an effort to keep awake.

Occasionally they could hear men shouting, then there would be no sound save the subdued hiss of steam. After a long wait a bell rang,

and Jawn's grasp tightened, but the other engine
gave only a few coughs and stopped again. The
ensuing silence was broken by Harvey stepping
to the tender and beckoning to the detective,
who had been sitting on the coal.

"All right," said Harvey. "We'll go ahead
and see what they're up to. You take the right
bank, and keep close to the edge where I can
talk to you if necessary." He swung out of the
cab and began laboriously to climb up the
seamed sloping rock, which reached a man's
height above the cab roof.

Excepting the occasional cracks and jagged
projections there was no foothold, and it was at
the expense of cut and scraped hands that he
scrambled up the soft limestone and reached
the top. He sat for a moment on the ground to
recover his breath and to pull himself together.
The detective was standing on the opposite bank
and Harvey rose and stumbled forward. They
crept along, climbing fences and tripping
through underbrush. As they rounded the
curve the ground began to slope away, and soon
they could see the headlight of an engine. Behind it, at the Sawyerville platform, stretched a
train of lighted cars.

Harvey and the detective had been talking across the cut, but now for the sake of caution they went on in silence. Harvey slipped around a farmyard that backed up to the track, and struck into the woods that lie north of Sawyerville almost up to the station and its lonely cluster of houses. Stepping quietly along a bridle path he soon came within earshot of the station.

Little knots of men stood on the platform talking excitedly. The new station agent and operator was running about in his shirt sleeves with his hand full of papers. Within the cars were crowds of men; Harvey estimated that there were several hundred. Standing near the engine, the centre of a small group, was a large man whom Harvey thought was McNally, but he could not be certain at that distance and in the uncertain light of flickering station lamps.

Harvey's sporting blood was up, and with entire forgetfulness of his exhaustion he crept slowly forward, worming through the brush and long grass behind a snake fence. Slowly he progressed until only a muddy road intervened between him and the north end of the platform. Taking advantage of a noisy blow-off from the

engine, he piled some brush up in front of him
and stretched out at full length with his chin on
his arm, viewing the scene through the opening between the two lowest rails of the fence.
Now he could easily recognize McNally, and
without being able to distinguish words could
even hear him talking. Suddenly McNally
stepped out from the group and called down the
platform, —

" Blake, are Wilkins and the boys back yet ? "

The reply was lost to Harvey, but McNally
shouted, —

" If they aren't here in five minutes, go
ahead."

That told Harvey just what he wanted to
know, and slowly turning he began crawling
back. But before he had gone very far, he
heard a sound which suggested possibilities. It
was the wheezing of his own engine at the
other end of the curve. Now that he stopped
to think, he realized that it must have been perfectly audible to McNally's party. From this
it was naturally to be inferred that " the boys "
had been sent out on a mission similar to his
own. It occurred to him that he and they
might have passed, and that the repassing might

not so easily be accomplished. He increased
his efforts and soon was deep enough in the
woods to get to his feet and run. When he
drew near the farmhouse he took a detour and
passed it with fifty yards to spare. He could
not afford to rouse any dogs. He was getting
into the open when three or four men appeared
directly in front of him, walking slowly from a
strip of woods toward the track. Harvey dug
his heel into the ground and dodged back, but
the men saw him and without a word started in
pursuit.

The chase was not a long one. Harvey was
completely hemmed in, and exhausted as he
was and spent with running, he was soon over-
hauled. He tried to call out, but one of the
men gripped his mouth.

Mallory, as soon as Harvey was out of sight,
settled down to await his return with more or
less impatience. The fireman leaned against
the forward end of the tender and promptly fell
asleep, but Jawn waked him with a growl,
whereupon the exhausted man stood erect,
struggling to bring his rebellious nerves under
control. As the minutes slipped by Jawn's

eyes shifted from track to bank and back to the cut again. The clouds that lingered from the afternoon rain hid every star save one near the horizon, which struggled to announce the coming dawn.

Ten minutes passed, and fifteen. Then came the warning bell of the other locomotive, followed by a quick succession of puffs as the big drivers gripped the rails. Jawn leaned far out the window and scanned the banks of the cut. No one was in sight. He ducked in and seized the throttle lever.

"Hold on," said Mallory. "Are they coming this way?"

"Yes."

Mallory seized his arm.

"Back up, then. We can't meet them."

Jawn jerked his elbow from Mallory's grasp and opened the throttle.

"Are you crazy, man!" Mallory shouted. "Stop her! You'll kill us!"

Jawn opened her a little wider. For an instant Mallory looked at him in wonder, then he sprang forward and jammed the lever close to the boiler.

"Reverse!" he ordered.

For reply Jawn turned on Mallory and crowded him back. Weak-nerved from the long strain, suffering for lack of sleep, the two men broke down for the moment, and struggled about the cab. The fireman stumbled back against the boiler with a dazed face, but after a moment he recovered and rushed between the two men.

"This ain't right!" he screamed. "If you two fight, we're ditched."

As he spoke, the detective who had gone with Harvey came slipping and tumbling down the cut, and clambered aboard the engine. Jawn and Mallory fell back against the opposite benches and glared at each other. Jawn suddenly reached for the throttle.

"Wait a minute," gasped Mallory; "she's stopped."

Half reluctantly Jawn listened. Sure enough, the other train had paused, evidently just around the curve.

"The man's right," Mallory went on. "We haven't got any business scrapping; we've got to pull together. Now tell me what you were trying to do."

Jawn looked out ahead before he replied, —

"I ain't going to leave Mr. West down there."

" Isn't Mr. West back ? " asked the detective, in a startled tone. " He's had time enough to go clear to the station and back. I went pretty near to it myself. They've got a train full of men. It looks like business."

"Hear that, Donohue?" said Mallory. "What do you think we can do against a gang like that?"

"That don't make no difference. Mr. Mattison says, 'Hold the line if you lose an engine doing it,' and I'm going to hold it."

" But stop to think, man. There isn't a possible chance of holding it. We'll do more good by dodging back and keeping them guessing until the relief comes. As it stands now we are perfectly helpless."

" Now look here," said Jawn. " You go back and fetch every man you got."

" What are you up to ? "

" No difference what I'm up to. You fetch your men."

Mallory looked sharply at Jawn, then he motioned to the detective, who dropped to the ground and hurried back.

" What's your plan ? " Mallory asked again. But Jawn shook his head and watched the cut.

In a moment the detective reappeared fol-

R

lowed by five others. All six came crowding upon the apron. Without leaving his seat Jawn gave his orders, —

"Get on the tender, as high up as you can, and when we go at 'em, yell like hell."

With startled, wondering faces the men clambered back, Mallory among them, taking positions on the tank and on what was left of the coal. From around the curve another succession of puffs drew Jawn's eyes to the front, and his grip tightened.

"Hold on, back there," he called, "and don't yell till I holler. Fire up, Billy."

Billy fired up and the engine moved slowly forward. She crept cautiously toward the curve, foot by foot. On the rock wall dead ahead a yellow light flashed, and then crept around toward them. Jawn waited until it was almost full in his eyes.

"Whistle, Billy," he said.

The hoarse whistle shrieked, and the other engine seemed to start, then hesitate.

"Now," said Jawn, without looking around, and he let out a tremendous yell of "At 'em, boys!" The men on the tender promptly raised an uproar, the fireman shouted as he jerked the whistle cord, and Jawn sat with one eye on the indicator, the other on the approaching head-light, his bass voice all the while roaring out a fiery challenge not unmixed with profanity.

The engineer of McNally's special had received no orders to sacrifice his engine, and had no desire to sacrifice himself. He wavered, stopped, then tried to back. But Jawn let out another notch, and rammed his bull nose into and through the other's pilot with such force that both locomotives left the track.

CHAPTER XVIII

THE COMING OF DAWN

THE collision occurred at the southern end of the cut. It had for the men in the C. & S. C. train the additional force of unexpectedness. It was not violent, as railway'collisions go, but the shock of it was enough to jerk the huddled, dozing men out of their seats, and to awaken them to a full consciousness that something had happened. In the stupefied hush which followed the crash they heard outside the train a chorus of shoutings, — derisive, blasphemous, triumphant. That completed their momentary demoralization; a panic swept them away, and the frenzied men fought each other in the effort to reach the car doors.

But the rush was checked as suddenly as it had begun. The first men to get through the doors had hardly leaped to the ground when they saw from the shadow of the cut the vicious spit of revolvers and heard the bullets singing

244

unpleasantly over their heads. Where they
stood the gray dawn made them perfectly
visible, but the blackness of the cut screened
their assailants and made it impossible to guess
their numbers. About twenty men had got
out of the C. & S. C. train when the volley was
fired, and the celerity with which they scattered brought another cheer from Mallory's
men intrenched in the cut.

Some of the fugitives scurried to the woods,
while others struggled back into the cars. The
shots had been heard inside the cars, and the
rush to get out of them was succeeded by
the impulse to lie down. The men were without leaders, without means of measuring the
peril they were in or the force of their opponents, without knowledge of what was expected
of them; and they lay cowering but angry in
the barricaded cars, awaiting further developments.

There was no one to tell them what to do.
Where were their leaders? The murmur ran
through the line of cars that McNally and
Wilkins had deserted them. For neither of
them was on the train when the collision
occurred.

McNally, standing on the Sawyerville platform near the rear end of his train, had already
given the signal to go ahead when a man came
out of the woods, hurried across the muddy
road, ran down the platform, and clutching
his arm said eagerly : —

" Mr. McNally, Wilkins wants you to come
over here. We've caught one of them and he
says he thinks it's the one you told him about."

McNally turned and shouted to the engineer,
" Hold on up there a minute " ; but the cry was
unheard, and the long train continued slowly
toward the curve. Smith, who had just brought
the report to McNally, started up the platform
in pursuit, but McNally stopped him.

" Never mind," he said. " They won't go
far. Now tell me about this fellow you've
caught. Where was he ? "

" Right over here in the woods; it's only
a little way. Wilkins wanted you should come
over there."

" Go ahead," said McNally. " Show me the
way."

The two men crossed the road and entered
the woods by the path. It was still as black as
midnight under the trees, and they felt their

way cautiously. Just north of the farmhouse they left the path and stepped into the crackling underbrush. They had gone but a few paces when they were stopped by the sound of a low whistle close by at their left.

"There they are," said the guide.

McNally started to follow him, but hesitated and then whispered: —

"I'll wait here. Send Wilkins out to me, will you?"

When Wilkins appeared McNally stepped back a little and looked around nervously before he spoke.

"Can they hear us?"

Wilkins shook his head.

"How much did you tell that young fellow of our conversation?" questioned McNally.

"Smith? Nothing but just what he told you. I said I thought he was the man you told me about."

"What does he look like?"

"Big man — straight dark hair. I took these out of his pockets."

They were a handful of papers, and McNally took them eagerly. "That's something like," he said.

It was too dark to make out anything, and he struck a match. The crackle was followed by another sound from the thicket, as though a man had moved suddenly and violently. McNally started and dropped the match, glancing suspiciously toward the spot whence the sound came.

"It's only the boys," said Wilkins. "Here, I'll give you a light."

As he sheltered the flickering match-light with his hands, McNally glanced over the papers. One of them he found by unfolding to be a map of the railroad. There were some memoranda, scrawled and unintelligible, and last of all, what appeared to be a note in a crumpled blue envelope, bearing a week-old postmark. He scrutinized it closely, and then rubbed his soft hands over it. There was the caricature of a smile on his face.

"That's all the light I need. He's the man."

As Wilkins dropped the match, McNally turned a little and slipped the blue note into his pocket. Then he handed the other papers to Wilkins, saying: —

"Put them back where you found them. We don't want to rob him."

In a moment, with lowered voice he went on : —

" I don't think it's necessary for me to give any further instructions. When you go back there just tell those men what we want. It's necessary that West shall be out of the game for the next day or two, that's all. I'll walk along toward the train, and when you get through with them follow me down the track. What force have they on the other train?"

" Not more than twenty men."

" That simplifies — "

As he started to speak there came to his ears a splintering crash followed by a quick succession of shots.

McNally smiled. " The boys are rushing things," he said. " I hope they aren't doing anything rash. I'll hurry along and pacify 'em. Follow me as soon as you can, will you?"

He turned to go, but Wilkins waited.

"Mr. McNally," he said, " I guess you'd better attend to that West business yourself. I'll send one of those men to you, and take Smith down to the train with me."

" What do you mean?"

" I guess you can see what I mean all right,"

said Wilkins. "I'd rather let you be responsible for any kidnapping."

He did not wait for a reply, but hurried into the thicket, and nodding to one of the men who still held Harvey he said in a low tone : —

"You're wanted out there.   Your partners can hold this chap all right."   Then with a gesture motioning Smith to follow, he felt his way through the woods and down the side of the cut to the track.

Once out of the shadow of the trees he could see plainly enough, for dawn was breaking fast.   The rear end of his train was in sight, about a hundred yards up the track; the head of it was hidden by the curve.   From the cut he could hear derisive shouts and cat-calls, but from his own train not a sound.   Puzzled and a little alarmed, he broke into a run.   He passed the rear cars and came around the curve in sight of the men in the cut.

"Get back there, you damned robber!" shouted one of them, and the command was followed by a shot.

The bullet went high over Wilkins's head, but it had its effect none the less.   He sprang up the steps of the nearest car and threw himself

against the door. It resisted his efforts, however, and from inside the car came another
warning, for a gruff voice said : —

"Quit that, if you don't want to be blown full
of holes."

Wilkins stepped out of line of the door before
he answered : —

"Let me in, you fool. It's me, Wilkins."

The door opened slowly and he looked into
the barrel of a levelled revolver, which was
lowered when he was recognized. He looked
about the crowded car in increasing amazement,
the men shifting sullenly under his glance. At
last he said : —

"What in hell are you men doing here?
Scared to death, too; and by half a dozen
men! Stand up now, and go out there and tie
'em up. It won't take you but a minute."

There was an inarticulate growl of protest, and
the man who had been guarding the door spoke :

"They've got us in a hole. We started to
get off the train and they shot at us from the
cut. They can pick us off like rabbits."

Wilkins hesitated. He did not know whether
or not the men in the cut would shoot to kill,
but he saw that their position gave them a tre-

mendous advantage in the first rush. He did
not care to face the responsibility of ordering a
charge that would prove too costly. After a
moment he said : —

"It'll be all right if you all do it together.
One of you speak to the men in the forward
cars and I'll go back and do the same thing.
Then when we give the signal make a rush."

Wilkins went through toward the rear of the
train, as he had said, but his object was to
gain time and to wait for McNally. Then the
responsibility could be shifted to where it belonged. When he reached the rear platform
he saw McNally coming up the track. He
hurried to meet him, and in a few words laid
the situation before him.

McNally's upper lip drew away from his
teeth as he heard it, but he spoke quietly.

"They've got us bluffed down, haven't they?
But I guess it's about time we called them.
They'll be pretty careful not to hit anybody
with those guns of theirs. Have the men come
through to the rear of the train and get off from
this platform where they'll be screened by the
curve. Then they can spread out through the
woods and come down on 'em from the sides of
the cut."

Of course the odds were overwhelming; they were greater even than the numerical disparity would indicate, for the men in the cut were utterly exhausted. They had staked everything on their bluff and had been sustained for a time by seeing that it was succeeding. But at last Jawn, standing in the cab of his derailed locomotive, saw something that made him call quickly to Mallory.

"They've started," he said.

"Where are they?"

"Comin' up through the woods."

Mallory glanced quickly about and said, "We're flanked. There's no good in staying here, is there?"

"The baggage car'll hold together for a while, and the other train ought to be here now."

"Well," said Mallory, "we'll try it. Come on, boys, get to cover."

The men climbed into the car, and Jawn and Mallory were discussing methods for defending it, when the fireman thought of something.

"How about Bill Jones?" he asked. "He's back with the flag. Ain't he liable to get snapped up?"

"He'll have to take his chances," said Mallory.

"Hold on, though.   It won't do for them to find him."

He glanced out of the window and then ran out on the platform.

"There's time enough, I guess," he muttered, turning and speaking into the car.   "I'm goin' back with him."

He disappeared, and Jawn quietly assumed command of the defences.   "Don't do any shooting," he said.   "It won't help any in this mix-up.   These are good to hit with," and he showed a coupling pin he held in his hand.

When the preparations were made for the defence, and all the bulky articles in the car had been placed where they would be most in the way of an attacking party, the men waited. They were stupid with fatigue, and even the prospect of an immediate attack failed to arouse them; but they were still game, and though they lay about the floor in attitudes of utter exhaustion their sullen determination to hold the car was unmistakable.

At last a shower of stones came rattling about the car, and they heard the shouts of two hundred men who came charging down the banks into the cut.   Jawn and his men breathed more freely now that the waiting was over, and drew themselves up with a spark of their old alertness. One man began singing, drumming on the car floor with a stick, —

"There'll be a hot time — "

and another, springing to his feet, took to balancing his loaded club, shifting it from finger to finger, and then catching it in his hand he struck quick and hard through the air to see where the grip was best.

Then they heard the sound of feet on the north platform, and some one tried the door. "Guess they're in here," they heard him say.

"Guess you'll find that you're dead right about that," observed the man who had been singing.

Jawn said no word, but waited with blazing eyes beside the door. He meant to strike the first blow with his coupling pin. There were two ineffectual thuds against the door and then a crash. The hinges started and one panel splintered inward. Another, and this time the door fell and a giant of a man, jerked off his balance by the sledge he had swung, staggered into the car. Jawn struck; the man's collar-bone crackled under the coupling pin and he fell forward with a yell. Then over him and over the fallen door came the rush. The handful of defenders chose their corners and fought in them, each in his own way; some in a sort of hysteria, screaming curses, some striking silently, and one, the singer, with a laugh on his lips. When the fireman was struck senseless, this man fought over him until forced back by press of numbers, so that he no longer had room to strike.

The defence of the baggage car was over, and the defenders, disabled and disarmed, were submitting to the handcuffs or to the bits of rope which were used in securing them, when there came a sound of cheering, which made their captors leave them hastily and clamber from the car. The relief had come.

It came on the run, with Mallory at the head. There was no order, no pretence at formation; simply a stream of eager, angry men, some running through the cut along the tracks, others stumbling through the woods above, all animated by the desire to reach the scene of action as quickly as possible. And waiting for them was another mob of men, the main body of McNally's army. They were crowded in the cut on both sides of the train they had just captured, with the knowledge rankling in their hearts that they had been held at bay by a handful of determined men. They were glad they had somebody to fight.

The moment the two bodies of men came together the confusion became indescribable. The men had no means of distinguishing between friend and foe. They were at too close quarters to make fighting possible, and if it had been, no one would have known whom to strike and whom to defend. The cut was densely packed with men who strained and swayed and struggled and swore, but who could not by any possibility fight. But slowly the increasing weight of the new arrivals began to tell, and slowly, almost imperceptibly, the mass began to move south. Eventually they would push out of the cut to the open, where they could discuss matters more satisfactorily.

In the excitement they did not hear the long train that came clanking up from the south and stopped just behind the C. & S. C. train. But a moment later the uproar ceased, as sounded

s

high and clear the echoing bugles, " Forward, Fours left into line, March ! " Looking, they saw six companies of the National Guard come swinging across the open, the horizontal rays of the rising sun gilding their fixed bayonets.

There was no need for shot or bayonet thrust, the mob was quiet. McNally, as he stood panting in the thickest of the crowd, knew what it meant. The time for violence was over; his army had outlived its usefulness. And he knew that however the fight for the M. & T. was to be won, this was the beginning of the end.

CHAPTER XIX

KATHERINE DECIDES

It was some hours before definite information was to be had concerning the present condition of affairs. No one knew whether his side had won or lost, whether the M. & T. was a Weeks road or a Porter road, though in the excitement each claimed control and made immediate efforts to enforce orders relating to its conduct. Messages flew back and forth along the singing wires, and wrecking trains started almost simultaneously from Manchester and from Truesdale, with instructions to clear up the muss at Sawyerville, in order that the regular train service be resumed.

But before matters were more than fairly under way, there came a sudden suspension of action. The Weeks wreckers paused at Brushingham, and contented themselves with pulling Harvey's first capture back on the rails. That done, the conductor stuffed a bundle of some-

what contradictory but imperative orders into
his pocket, and stretched himself on the little
red bench on the Brushingham station platform; the engineer, after a shouted order, settled down to the nearest approach to rest
known to an engineer on duty; the division car
repairer and the roadmaster curled up in the
caboose, for they had been routed out at an
unseemly hour; the station agent amused himself reading the messages that rattled through
to the South and back, telling of a muddle at
headquarters.   When a wrecking train is held
for orders, it is safe to assume that something
has happened.

Down the line there was a similar occur-
rence.   The Truesdale repair crew was caught
at Sawyerville and ordered back.   But before
the astonished conductor had read the message
through, another came ordering him on, subject
no longer to the Superintendent's orders, but to
those of Colonel Wray, 3d N. G.

The Governor of the State, in the conduct of
routine matters, was usually content to follow
precedent, which means that the State House
clerical force was let more or less severely alone
to govern the community, while the executive

directed the politics of his party with a view to coming elections. At times an emergency occurred, miners struck, excited citizens lynched a negro, henchmen of the other party strained the voting laws, municipal corporations endeavored to steal State privileges — in any of which cases he delayed definite action until public sentiment bayed at his heels, then he acted with shrewdness and despatch. At the time of the fight, this same noisy public was keen on the scent of the railroads. Certain street railway corporations had called out abuse by methods which were excusable only for their success, and the mass saw no reason to believe that one corporation was better than another. Discriminating freight tariffs, which had seemed to favor a neighboring State, had thoroughly antagonized the country districts — and the country districts' vote. From even the solid communities had come rumors of restlessness and discontent. Ward bosses were worried, county magnates were dodging reform committees instigated by the traditionally conscientious minority, and the Governor knew that certain bills which awaited his signature were not likely to increase his following.

So it was that the great man was watching, watching and waiting, for the opportunity to strike a blow which should swing public sentiment around in his favor. Up to the present the whole State had been quiet. The miners were as orderly as the Sunday-school over which he presided when in his native town. The great labor organizations he was so eager to conciliate perversely gave him no opportunity.

And so it was that when messages came pouring in upon him from bosses and chairmen and advisers urging immediate interference in the M. & T. fight, when the sheriff of Malden County sent in an hysterical report, all instigated by the pungent advices from mad and muddy Senator Sporty Jones — the Governor inclined his ear. He was a shrewd man, and he knew that in order to make a distinct impression on The Public his blow must be sudden and spectacular. The longer he thought on it, the more the opportunity pleased him, and before the evening was far advanced Colonel Wray was speeding to Truesdale.

The Third was not a city regiment. It was made up of men from the middle sections of the

State, a company to every few counties with
battalion headquarters in three of the smaller
cities, Truesdale for one. In the city regiments
was a blue-stocking element which did not fit
the Governor's present needs.

As soon as Colonel Wray reached Truesdale,
he established himself in the inhospitable ware-
house which in reports was called an armory.
Before midnight the local company was collected, uniformed, and in order. Later special
trains arrived, and squads and companies
marched through the echoing streets, to sit dozing about the armory. At three-thirty a train
came in from the southern counties bringing
the second battalion, three hundred husky farm
lads who glowed with responsibility as they
stacked arms and awaited orders.

Then came a telephone message that Mc-
Nally's relief train had left for the North.
Colonel Wray waited no longer but marched
over to the station, seized the telegraph office
and the telephone, placed guards at each entrance and about the train shed, ordered the
yard master to make up another train, levied on
the station restaurant for six hundred cups of
coffee, and tore fly-leaves from the news-stand

books to write special orders for the waiting adjutant.

Meanwhile Porter was feverish. He tried to bulldoze the sergeant in the telegraph office only to be hustled off by a corporal's guard. He finally reached the Colonel's ear, but was heard in courteous silence. He made an effort to call up the Oakwood Club to send a message to McNally, but the sunburned young fellow in the 'phone box leaned on his rifle and shook his head. The same thing happened when he tried to get out of the building — "Sorry, sir. Captain's orders" — and the baffled magnate paced up and down the waiting room between long files of light-hearted boys in blue. It was humiliating to consider that he had subscribed heavily toward fitting up the Truesdale armory, that half the officers knew him and feared his influence.

While he was racking his brain sudden orders were shouted through the building. The lounging groups came up with a jerk, there was a rattle of arms, and in ten seconds the farm boys had resolved into a machine, a set of rigid blue lines that reached the length of the waiting room. There was another order, and one after another the companies broke into columns of twos and swung through the glass doors, which were held open by a couple of scared but admiring waiters.

Porter followed the last company and stood in the doorway behind two crossed rifles watching the troops climb into the cars. The Colonel stood at the track gate as the men marched through, talking with his aids. Porter thought for a moment of calling to him, but realized the futility of it after the treatment he had just received. Besides, even a railroad president could hardly keep his dignity with those ridiculous guns under his nose. So he turned and walked slowly to his temporary headquarters in the station agent's office, but to find that the young captain left in command by Colonel Wray had made himself at home and was issuing orders to a snub-nosed lieutenant.

Porter took a chair and looked out of the window. For a moment he was too weary to be aggressive. Worry and loss of sleep had lined his face, and the absence of news from McNally kept his nerves strung. As he sat there gripping the arms of the chair, face a little flushed, hair disarranged, collar dusty, he looked ten years past his age. It was a critical moment in the fight, and he knew it, but cornered as he was, absolutely uninformed as to his position in the struggle, or the meaning of the military display, a sense of helplessness almost unnerved him. Heretofore his fights had been largely conducted through deferential employees. He was accustomed to bows and scrapes, to men who feared him, who watched his every move in awe, and to find himself utterly at the mercy of these tin soldiers was disgusting. It was twenty-four hours since he had had a wink of sleep and eighteen since he had eaten a full meal — facts which in no small measure lessened the stability of his mental poise. And there he sat waiting through the darkness and the dawn.

The reds and golds in the eastern sky spread and paled. The little green-clad city stretched down the gentle hill, now indistinct in the haze. An early electric car whirred and jangled past the station, and Porter was half conscious of the noise. He got up, straightened his stiff joints, and went to the lunch counter, where he had to jostle between two gawky privates before he could order a cup of smoky cereal coffee and a sandwich. After getting a place he could not eat, so he returned to the office. Now that some sort of routine was established, the Captain showed a willingness to meet him civilly.

" See here," said Porter, after a few commonplaces had been exchanged, " how long is this
going to keep up? There is no sense in holding me here."

"Sorry, sir. I have no desire to inconvenience you, but my orders are to let no one out
and no one in. And you know what orders are
for."

"Oh, that's all right," — Porter leaned back
in his chair and looked out the window, — " but
there's such a thing as going to extremes. Sometimes common sense supersedes orders."

"You forget, Mr. Porter, that you are here
for the purpose of conducting a raid, and we are
here to stop that raid. Under the circumstances
it is my duty to hold you and every one connected
with the affair until I am otherwise ordered."

" But I am not a thief, man."

" No, perhaps not." The Captain turned to
some papers on the desk, and Porter continued
to look out, wearily, with a sudden dull ache
above his eyes.

A corporal appeared in the doorway, saluting.

" There's a young lady, sir, says she's got to
see Mr. Porter."

" Who is she?"

"Don't know, but she sticks to it."

"It's my daughter," said Porter, with an effort to rise. "Where is she?"

"Wait," the Captain said; "I'll speak to her," and he followed the soldier.

Porter sat still. After a little he heard voices in the waiting room, and Katherine entered the office. At the sight of his worn, haggard face her annoyed expression vanished, and she drew the Captain's chair beside her father's and laid her hand upon his forehead.

"You are sick," she said gently.

"Nonsense" — he made a feeble effort to shake off her hand — "I asked you not to come back. I'm tired, that's all."

Katherine rose and looked about.

"Come into the waiting room, dad, and lie down. You must have some sleep or you won't be good for anything."

"You must go back," said Porter, shaking his head. "This is no place for you."

Katherine looked quietly into his eyes. It was not the first time that the strain of his busy life had told upon her father's nerves, and she knew what was the matter.

"Come, dad," she said. "Get a little sleep,

and I'll stay by and wake you if there is any news."

Porter scowled, then slowly rose. The Captain, who had been hesitating in the doorway, came forward to assist. Porter turned on him savagely. "Let me alone. I can walk, I guess." But at a glance from Katherine the Captain took an arm, and Porter submitted, seemingly unconscious of his inconsistency.

Along the walls of the waiting room were benches, and on one of these they tried to make Porter comfortable. When she saw that his head must rest on the wooden seat, Katherine hesitated and looked at the Captain, who was following her with his eyes.

"I wish there was something for a pillow," she said. "Perhaps" — she stood erect and looked slowly about the waiting room, then stepped to the door of the office, returning with a pretty frown. "I wonder" — she met the Captain's gaze smiling frankly — "if you would let me take your coat."

He was not an old officer, and he was not a hermit, so with but slight hesitation he unbuckled his belt, removed the coat, rolled it up, and as Katherine raised her father's head he slipped it underneath.

"Will you send one of your men to a drug store for some camphor?" said Katherine, fumbling in the purse that hung from her belt.

The Captain beckoned to one of the soldiers who were clustered about the door, and placed him at Katherine's disposal. When he returned she soaked her handkerchief with the camphor and laid it on her father's forehead. He was already asleep.

"He'll be better as soon as he has had a little rest," Katherine said. "You are very good to help us." The Captain bowed with the expression of a man who has just been promoted, but said nothing.

For an hour Porter slept, and during that time Katherine stayed by him, moistening the folded handkerchief and chafing his wrists. The Captain, his importance and self-command oozing away a bit at a time as he watched the cool, quiet girl, hovered near as often as his dignity would permit with offers of assistance, most of which Katherine accepted. He put her horses and trap in charge of a militiaman, he brought out a rocking-chair for her, and when, a little after eight o'clock, Porter showed signs of waking, he sent out for some breakfast.

On Porter, the touch of sleep, the welcome cup of coffee, and more than anything else his daughter's soothing presence, seemed to have a marked effect. He sat up, leaning back heavily, and with a struggle collected his thoughts. Katherine joked with him, and fussed over him with a maternal solicitude that made the Captain smile.

At eight-thirty, as Porter was sipping another cup of coffee, the corporal appeared.

"A man says he's got to see Mr. Porter, sir. A Mr. McNally."

"McNally," cried Porter, starting up only to sink back, breathing heavily. "Bring him here. I've got to see him."

The Captain hesitated.

"Did he state his business?"

"No, sir. But he has a pass through the lines at Sawyerville, signed by Colonel Wray."

"Um — let him come in."

It was not the Mr. McNally who had played for Katherine two nights before. That had been a well-groomed, self-possessed man of the world; this was a muddy, unshaven, angry man, who spoke in a loud voice and smothered an oath just too late to keep it from her ear.

He recovered somewhat, but even McNally could not lose sleep and temper for so many hours without a more or less immediate result. As she looked at him with a cool bow, Katherine thought of Harvey, and something caught in her throat.

"Well," said Porter, "what about it? What's happened? Who's running this road?"

McNally looked curiously at the Captain before he replied. That officer, at an appealing glance from Katherine, left the group.

"The Governor is running it. He's played a game that knocks us silly. He's come down on us and cinched things for the senatorship at one crack."

"What do you mean?" In his excitement Porter sat erect.

"The Old Man has declared the M. & T. under military rule until the courts choose to settle it to suit themselves. That throws us out, throws Weeks out, and the devil take the hindmost."

"Has there been trouble?"

"They smashed into us at Sawyerville"—he suddenly remembered Katherine—"Excuse me, Miss Porter, I must see your father alone."

" He cannot be excited, Mr. McNally."

" There is no time to waste — "

Katherine turned abruptly and went into the office.

"Yes," said McNally, "they ripped into us at Sawyerville and we had the hell of a time till Wray's guards came up and stopped it. Wray let me through, — it was just after daylight, — and I picked up a horse from a farmer and rode down. But we got West though, damn him! — caught him sneaking through the bushes."

" Be careful, McNally, we've got to be careful. It's no time to get mixed up in a thing like that — we — we can't afford — "

"That's all right, Porter. We don't know where he is — I don't know, you don't know — and before we find out he'll be loose again."

"But — Jim — Weeks don't forget that kind of thing, McNally — Jim Weeks — "

"Oh, damn Jim Weeks! I'll take care of him."

Porter paused to drink at a gulp what was left of his coffee.

"Remember, McNally, I can't back you if you get careless — I can't back you, you know."

T

"God, man! you've got to back me! You've got to back me through everything, or you'll go down with me. I tell you, Porter, we're too far in to back out, and it's nerve that's going to win. If you don't back me, if you don't draw on every cent you've got to shove it through, you'll be the one to be hit — not me." He paced the floor. "Yes, sir. It's you if it's anybody." Suddenly he stopped. He looked hard at Porter, then he turned quickly and strode into the office. Katherine was standing at the window.

"Miss Katherine — "

"Mr. McNally, my name is Miss Porter."

"Miss — Miss Porter, I met a friend of yours this morning. I met him under peculiar circumstances. We had some words, I regret to say, and he left this with me." The plump, dirty hand drew a blue envelope from McNally's coat pocket. "It has seemed to me that where your father's honor was as seriously involved as in this matter, you should have followed some other course than that of traitor."

In his excitement, McNally misunderstood Katherine's silence.

"You have deliberately drawn out your

father and me that you might aid our opponents.
I have watched you — I have seen it — it is not
your fault that we are not ruined — and for the
sake of a man that I caught spying on us this
morning, sneaking through the bushes in the
dark — "

There was a groan from the doorway. Porter
stood there with one hand over his eyes. Katherine looked for an instant, then she brushed
past McNally, and with one arm about her
father she called to the Captain, who stood at
the other side of the waiting room. He came
at once.

"Captain," she said, "I must ask you to take
care of my father. Please telephone for a
doctor and a closed carriage, and see that he is
sent home at once. I shall drive there in the
trap to prepare for him. Don't let this man"
— she turned contemptuously toward McNally
— "speak to him or excite him in any way.
Will you do this?" As she spoke her face
softened, and she held out her hand. The Captain took it.

"Yes, Miss Porter, I will take care of him."

Katherine, without looking again at McNally,
walked to the door and called for her trap. As

she waited on the steps, a newsboy came running down the walk, crying : —

"Nine o'clock Extry! All 'bout M. & T. riot!"

Katherine stopped him and bought a paper. The black headings told the story tersely, but one item stood out with vivid distinctness. She read, "Harvey West Disappears — Supposed that He Was Kidnapped — His Followers Swear Vengeance — Rumored that He Is Hidden Near The Oakwood Club." For a moment the blood left her face, and her nerves tightened, but when the trap was pulled up she was herself, and the smile she gave the soldier in charge brought forth an earnest but amateurish salute.

Then Katherine drove home — it was her duty to go home. But, her duty done, she would drive straight to the Oakwood Club.

CHAPTER XX

HARVEY

BEFORE the dawn broke on Thursday morning Harvey was a prisoner. It was so absurd, so ridiculously theatrical, that had he not been too tired to think clearly, his sense of humor would have been equal to the occasion; as it was, he was angry, baffled, desperate. While held in the thicket by Wilkins's gang he had caught a voice too like McNally's to be easily mistaken, and when McNally struck the match that showed him the papers, Harvey had with an effort flopped over on the leaves, bound as he was, and through the bushes had caught a glimpse of McNally's face and figure.

While the shooting and the uproar sounded from the cut Harvey was held in the woods, but before the second encounter his captors jerked him to his feet, tied his handkerchief across his eyes, and led him stumbling away. In a few moments Harvey lost all sense of direction. He figured that he was still on the east side of the track, and in all probability was going southeast on the river road. For a short while he tried to keep the direction, but realizing that he might be turned without knowing it, he gave up and decided to rely upon a chance opportunity to escape. Undoubtedly his guards were acting simply as agents, and it occurred to him that he might be able to influence them; but as his occasional attempts at conversation brought only profanity in reply, he fell back upon silence.

Through his thin bandage he could feel that the light was growing brighter. Then he was led from the road, splashing through a ditch and sprawling over another fence. He bumped into a tree. The men jerked him roughly away and led him forward, twisting and stepping from side to side. Occasionally his foot struck a fallen log. Evidently they were in a heavy wood.

At best their progress was very slow and was marked with numerous haltings and delays. Finally, about two hours after the start, Harvey was thrust through a doorway and a lock clicked behind him. He tore off the handkerchief and found himself in a small office, evidently deserted, for the rusted stove, the broken chair, and the floor were thickly coated with dust. There was one window, empty of glass and boarded up from the outside. He looked through a crack and saw the caved-in shaft house and the straggling waste heap of a worked-out mine. "Wonder how long they're going to try this game," he thought. He picked up the remains of a chair and tipping it over sat on the rounds.

Harvey was nearly done for. Aside from the strain of the week, and particularly of the night just ended, he was wet to the knees, and his head ached from a chance blow received during his brief struggle near the Sawyerville station. His eyelids drooped, and for fear of dropping off to sleep he rose and walked the floor. Gradually his head cleared. It occurred to him that McNally would have run the risk involved in kidnapping him only because it was very important he should be gotten out of the way. Therefore, he reasoned, it was equally important from his point of view that he remain decidedly in the way. He looked through the crack and saw three men standing a few yards from the window talking excitedly. Their voices were gradually rising.

"What you goin' to do with him?" asked one. "We can't keep him here."

"Well, it's only for a few days."

"But who's goin' to feed him?"

"Yes," said the third, "an' how about us?"

"Oh, you'll be all right," from the big man, who seemed to be the leader; "that's all fixed."

"Who's goin' to do it — McNally?"

"Ssh!" the leader looked around, and all three lowered their voices.

Finally they seemed to reach an agreement; for the first speaker turned and walked rapidly toward the woods, and the others took to patrolling the small building.

Again Harvey walked the floor. If he was to be of any service to Jim Weeks during what was left of the fight, it was absolutely necessary that he escape as soon as possible. In the course of his work as Jim's private secretary he had become fairly well acquainted with the details of his employer's many interests. Nearly all the mines along the M. & T. were owned or controlled by the capital which Jim represented, and Harvey knew the location of each of these. There was but one abandoned mine in the Sawyerville district, the Valley Shaft; it was about four miles from Sawyerville station and perhaps three or four from the Oakwood Club.

Therefore, he reasoned, if he once broke loose
from this galling restraint, he would soon be in a
position to communicate with Jim.

Outside, the big man stood directly before the
window; his fellow could be heard walking to
and fro in the rear of the building. Harvey
looked about the room. There was nothing to
serve as a weapon, except some part of the
stove. He bent down and removed one of the
small iron legs, taking care to make no noise.
Then he examined the window. The boards
were half-inch stuff, nailed on with little idea of
security, probably because the office contained
nothing worth stealing. He figured that it
would be no difficult matter for a man of his
weight and strength to force an exit. For the
moment he forgot his weariness.

Accordingly he drew back across the room,
and bracing for a second against the wall, he
ran forward and threw himself at the boards.
They gave way more easily than he had supposed, and a rapid effort landed him squarely
on the leader, who had turned at the noise.
The struggle was short. Each had received a
few hard blows when the man jerked his right
arm loose and reached back for his revolver.

Harvey took advantage of his open guard to
strike a quick blow with the stove leg and
brought the fellow to the ground.   Harvey
rolled him over, took the revolver from his
pocket, and picked up his own hat.   A noise
from behind the building called to mind the
other man, and he hurried forward.   The other
was walking stealthily toward the shaft house.

"Say," called Harvey.

The man turned sullenly.

"Your friend there — he doesn't feel well,"
Harvey laughed nervously and gestured with
the revolver; "you'd better look after him.
I've got to go now."   He paused to glance back
at the big man, who was lying on one elbow and
rubbing his head, then he turned and ran
toward the woods.

Once on the way, however, Harvey's sudden
nervous strength deserted him.   One of his
opponent's blows had cut his scalp, and he was
surprised to feel blood trickling down his face.
He ran until his breath gave out, then he walked,
struggling to overcome the dizziness that was
coming on him.   After going some distance he
found a bridle path, and soon saw the river road
before him.   The need of hurry urging him on, he

left the path to cut across a meadow. With some difficulty he drew himself upon the fence, and paused for breath with one leg thrown over the top rail. Then he felt a wave of dizziness, and, his muscles relaxing, he pitched forward into the long grass.

Good nursing, proper food, and a brief rest were enough to pull together Porter's yielding nerves. There was some delay at first in getting a physician, and Katherine was obliged to wait for the greater part of an hour before the slowly driven carriage brought her father home. Considerable time passed before his improvement justified her in leaving the house, and then it was so near noon that she decided to wait until after lunch.

Once on the road behind Ned and Nick, and beside the erect groom, Katherine realized the delicacy of the situation. Up to this moment she had been acting frankly upon impulse. It was so clear to her mind that McNally had been instrumental in the kidnapping of Harvey, and the sudden emotion aroused by the whole affair had so overwhelmed her, that for the time her only thought had been to get to Har-

vey, to be near him and of some service to him.
But Katherine's impulse on this occasion was
not far in advance of her reason, and what had
begun in a whirl of excitement was continued in
a spirit of quiet persistence.   To be sure, there
was a moment of wavering, but even then she
did not think seriously of turning back.   Anyway, there was nothing marked or unusual in
frequent drives to the club during this crisp
golfing weather.

It was after two o'clock when she reached the
club.   The links were dotted here and there
with golfers, and the usual autumn quiet hung
about the verandas and halls of the building,
but in the office there was bustle and excitement.
Katherine stood near the wide fireplace in the
lower hall drawing off her gloves and looking
through the office door.   A man was telephoning,
a big man with a quiet voice.   In a moment he
rang off and turned around.   His face interested
Katherine and she watched him as he talked to
the steward; she could not help hearing the
conversation.

" I've got to have another horse," the big man
was saying.   " I'll pay you whatever your time
is worth.   I want this whole county stirred up
in half an hour."

"But, sir, I cannot leave the club. We are short of help as it is, and the caddies are busy."

"I've no time to talk. A man has been kidnapped and very likely injured. You get a rig — any kind, a farm wagon, if the horses are good — and have it here in fifteen minutes. Figure your time at whatever you like and send the bill to me."

He handed a card to the steward, who looked at it with a slight start, and murmuring, "Certainly, Mr. Weeks," started down the hall. Katherine stopped him.

"What is it, Perry?"

"Jim — Mr. Weeks. He wants a horse."

"You may lend him my trap — And, Perry, say nothing of it." Without waiting for a reply, she went into the reading room, picked up a magazine, and, throwing open her jacket, sat on the broad window-seat. A moment later Ned and Nick were pulled up on the drive, Jim Weeks climbed in beside the groom, and they hurried down toward the bridge.

The magazine lay open in Katherine's lap. She rested an elbow on the window-sill and sat for a long time looking out across the valley. Not two weeks before this day she had stood

on the veranda with Harvey, looking at the
same picture through the haze of twilight.
Then it had seemed like summer; now it was
unmistakably autumn. Then the leaves were
only beginning to yield to the touch of the waning year; now they were aflame and dropping
— as she looked a whirl of them danced across
the sloping lawn, the stragglers settling in the
grass already marked by little dabs of red and
russet brown. Farther off, in the valley, were
corn-fields, now squares of yellow and bronze
and gold. It was a glowing picture, but to
Katherine it meant only that summer was dead,
and she viewed it with vague regret.

The afternoon wore on, but Katherine took
no account of it. At a little after four, when
Jim Weeks drove up and entered the building,
she was startled into looking at her watch.
She heard the telephone bell ring, and realized
that he was talking. Then he paced up and
down the hall. She wanted to go out there and
ask him about Harvey, whether he was found,
or whether — she shuddered a little at the
thought of injury — but a feeling of helplessness possessed her. She realized that the time
was slipping rapidly away. Jim Weeks might

go, and she would have learned nothing, would have done nothing. But she had not come altogether in vain. She recalled with half-defiant pride that Jim had used her horses.

" You are Miss Porter ? "

Katherine started, and turned with a slow blush. Weeks stood gravely looking at her.

" I understand that I have to thank you," he continued. " They were your horses, I believe. I hope I have not inconvenienced you by keeping you here. But it was an emergency."

" Has Mr. West been found ? " Katherine struggled to keep the anxiety out of her voice.

" No." Weeks sat down. " It seems impossible to get any word. I've roused things pretty effectively though, I think. There's a reward up. The sheriffs of both counties are at work, and the farmers are all stirred up. There's nothing to do but wait. If he's found, and by any chance is hurt, they're to bring him here."

" Wouldn't it be a good plan to have a doctor here, in case — "

" I don't think it is necessary. Of course the probability is that he is locked up somewhere and is being held for a day or so. If he

is knocked out, it was not done intentionally.
They wouldn't dare."

At the word "they" Katherine winced a
little, but Weeks apparently was entirely impersonal.   There was a silence, Weeks sitting with
slightly drawn brows but with an otherwise impassive face, Katherine looking out the window.
A little later a wagon came slowly up the road-
way.   Two men were on the seat and a third
reclined in the box.   They were driving carefully, and Jim did not hear the sound of the
wheels until a subdued exclamation from Katherine drew his attention.   She was sitting erect,
her hands gripping a cushion.   Jim followed
her gaze, then without a word he rose and hurried from the room.

A moment later Katherine saw the wagon
pull up at the steps, Weeks running down to
meet it.   The man beside the driver dropped
back into the wagon box and raised the reclin-
ing figure ; then he and Jim helped him to the
ground.

In spite of the soiled clothes, the matted hair,
and the bandage across the forehead, Katherine
recognized Harvey.   When she saw that he
could walk, even though leaning heavily on the

others, her heart bounded. The three came slowly up the steps. Then she could hear Jim's voice in the hall, evidently issuing an order, and the steward slid one of the hall settees into the room and piled rugs upon it.

Katherine rose in some doubt as they entered. She had taken up two of the cushions, one in each hand, and stood holding them. By now it was nearing five o'clock. The sun was about setting, and while outdoors it was still light, the long low room was already dim with approaching evening, so that not until he was close at hand could she see Harvey distinctly. But when she did distinguish the pale face and the weary eyes, her hesitation vanished and she hastened to lay the cushions on the settee. Harvey evidently had not observed her, for he suddenly drew back.

"Really, Miss Porter, I'm not such an invalid as these people are trying to make out. I don't need to lie down." He laughed slightly as Jim drew him forward. "It's just a little stiffness. See here—" he broke away from his helpers and walked somewhat uncertainly to the settee, sitting on the edge. "What's the matter with that?"

U

" Lie down, West," said Jim, quietly. Katherine glanced at him quickly. It was a peremptory order, but delivered in a quiet friendly tone whose calm assertiveness admitted of no debate. With an impatient gesture Harvey obeyed. Indeed, as Katherine looked almost shyly at this big, self-contained man she wondered if it would be possible to disobey him. And with the sudden realization of his secure authority came a wave of pity for her own father, the man who had thrown himself against this human rock and who was suffering for it. She turned away an instant for fear that her face would reveal her emotion.

" Well," said Jim, looking at his watch, " by starting now I can catch the early train to Chicago. Be careful, West; there's no hurry. I'll wire you in the morning if there is anything important. Miss Porter, may I ask you to see that the steward takes care of Mr. West? I'll send a doctor out. I'm sorry to trouble you — there's no one else."

Katherine inclined her head. And then she realized that Harvey and she were alone.

" Won't you draw up a chair? " said Harvey. " I want to talk to you. I'm glad you're here.

It's an awful bore to be alone when you're this way."

His attempt at an easy manner gave Katherine a sense of relief. She sat beside him.

"I'm sorry you are hurt. How did it happen?"

"I think I fell off a fence. Wonder if I lost my handkerchief?" He thrust his hand into his pocket, and drew out a revolver, clasping it by the barrel. "That's funny. I don't remember — oh, yes." He stuffed it back into his pocket.

"What is it? Tell me about it."

Harvey looked thoughtfully at her. It occurred to him that to let her know of McNally's actions, which presumably were instigated by Porter himself, would be bringing matters too close home.

"No," he replied, "it's rather a disagreeable story. If you were a good nurse you would try to make me forget it. I'm glad you are here — very glad. How did you happen to come?"

"I often drive out. It is growing dark. I must think about getting back."

"No," said Harvey, quickly, "don't go. I don't want you to go. I want to talk to you."

His voice dropped as he spoke, and both suddenly became conscious of a change that had come over them, between them. Katherine sat still, turning her head toward the window, and though she could not see him she knew that Harvey was looking at her. The room was darker now.

"Have you thought how odd this is," Harvey went on, "this conversation? We are talking just as though nothing had happened, just as though we were the same people who — who bought things at Field's; but we aren't. There's no use in thinking we are." He paused to raise himself on his elbow. "Do you know it is just twelve days since we were here?"

Katherine laughed a little.

"You have counted them?"

"Yes. Last night when I was coming down on the special I thought about it — you know it seems longer, it seems a year ago. You remember we talked about the M. & T. And the next day when you drove me to the station — do you remember? I've wondered since then, a good many times, what you meant, whether you really wanted to see us win." She started to speak, but he broke in: "If I dared think so — "

"You think I am weak."

"No, if you really want to know what I think — I think you are the strongest girl I ever knew. Katherine," — he reached impulsively for her hand, but she drew it away, — "I think you are — well, I might as well say it, you probably know it anyhow. I love you. I — I don't know that there is anything else to say."

Katherine leaned back and looked at him. Her back was toward the window, and he could see only the outline of her head.

"Are you sure?" she asked slowly.

"You mean — you think I'm not well, that I haven't control of myself — I do love you, Katherine, so much that I can't get along without you. You believe me, don't you? You must believe me!"

"Yes," very slowly, "I believe you."

"Then — "

"I don't know what to say. I'm afraid I — Oh, don't say any more! It isn't right." She rose suddenly as if to move away, but Harvey caught her dress and then her hand.

"Katherine, you aren't going to leave me this way. Perhaps you don't want me, perhaps I have been mistaken and foolish, but I love you, and that ought to count for something."

"It does — you don't understand — " She looked out the window for a moment: the first low-lying stars were out. " Don't you suppose," she said at last, in a labored voice, " that I have feelings? Don't you suppose that I — I don't mean that, either. You have been fighting my father — I have helped you. I have helped you to injure him, my own father. He is sick now, and I left him to-day, because — " Harvey's grasp tightened. " I have been disloyal to him, I have been dishonest — and that counts for something, too. No — we have been good friends, we can still be good friends. Perhaps, if it had been different — but it wasn't."

"You don't mean this, Katherine."

She drew her hand away and stood erect, dignified now and calm.

"I am going home. I know that you love me, and I know that you will not hurt me any longer; for it does hurt me, I will tell you that."

"But I shall see you — " With an effort, he raised himself to his feet and stood, weak and giddy, leaning on the back of the chair. "I won't give you up!"

"Lie down. You mustn't tire yourself. We

don't know what may happen," she steadied
his arm as he sat down on the couch; "we
only know what is right for us now. Good-by.
I will speak to the steward."

With throbbing head Harvey sank back on
the cushions. A few moments later the doctor
came in.

CHAPTER XXI

THE TILLMAN CITY STOCK

THE Governor was a familiar figure in Chicago, and his presence in a hotel lobby ordinarily excited no more than a glance of curious interest from the loungers about the news stand. The sensation he caused, when he entered the office of the Great Northern on Friday afternoon, was due to the company he brought with him; for on one side walked a pale, nervous, careworn man, who was hardly recognizable as the dapper, self-contained William C. Porter, and on the other, burly as ever, and, though grave, confident as ever, was Jim Weeks.

A man who was registering at the desk watched them as they stepped into an elevator, and then said to the clerk : —

" Have you got your furniture well insured? Because you can bet your life the fur will begin to fly in a few minutes."

296

But the conference, which any reporter in Chicago would have given his ears to hear, was a quiet one. The Governor dominated the situation, and at the very outset he made this clear. In his dealings with the Intelligent Voter he was wont to call a spade by many high-sounding names, but when he chose he could call it a spade, and he did choose so to do this afternoon.

The road, he said, was for the present in the hands of the State. Every station was guarded by a detail of State troops who had instructions to pay no attention to any writs from any court whatever. In every case they were to respect actual possession, and to allow the routine work of running the road to be carried on by the men they found in charge. This state of things would continue until the Governor was fully convinced that there would be no further attempt by either party to obtain possession of the road by force.

The Governor went on to point out that a continuation of this arrangement was against the interest of both parties, as it brought the affairs of the road into unpleasant prominence, and every added day of it antagonized the peo-

ple more, and might eventually lead to some
rather drastic legislation which would hurt every
road in the State.

The courts would of course settle the question of possession in time, but meanwhile some
sort of an understanding must be reached.
The Governor proposed as a solution of the
difficulty that the two men should jointly sign
a paper he had drawn up.

It was a petition addressed to the Governor
himself, asking him to appoint one or more men
to act as receivers of the road until the suits
should be settled by the regular process of law.
The men to be appointed were to be allies of
neither party in the fight.   Both parties agreed
to refrain from any further attempts to use
force in getting possession of the road.

Weeks readily, and Porter after a moment of
hesitation, signed the paper, and the Governor
announced that his appointment would be made
immediately.

It was then arranged that the regular annual
election of directors, which was due on the following Tuesday, should be held as usual.   After
the legal questions were settled, the Governor's
commission would turn over the road to the
newly elected board.

When the conference was over, and it had not been a long one, the two warring railway magnates, who in the past week had set the whole State by the ears, rose and politely took their leave. As they went down in the elevator together, Weeks remarked, —

"Autumn seems to have taken hold early this year."

"Yes," answered Porter, "it's extremely disagreeable weather. I have my carriage here. May I save you a walk?"

"No, thanks," said Jim; "I'm not going far."

When they parted at the door they did not shake hands, but there was nothing in their manner to indicate that they had not just met for the first time at an afternoon tea.

Jim went straight to his office, told Pease that he must not be disturbed, and settled himself to some hard thinking. That afternoon had materially changed the situation, and had for the most part simplified it. There was no further necessity for guarding against force. There was no longer anything to be apprehended from the legal juggling of Judge Black, for the Governor's interposition had rendered

him quite harmless. When the case was tried
it would be before an unprejudiced court. The
seizure of the road by the militia had come at the
right moment for Jim, for it left his employees
in possession as far down as Sawyerville.

The longer Jim thought, the simpler the problem became. He must bring about the election
of his board of directors. As matters stood he
could accomplish this only by voting the nine
thousand shares of new stock he had issued the
week before, thus giving Porter a more or less
strong case against him. But if he could command a majority of the stock without this, there
would be absolutely nothing for the courts to
decide, and Tuesday evening would see him
completely victorious. And so, for the first
time that week, Jim turned the whole force of
his attention to the Tillman City stock.

It was just ten days since he had instructed
Bridge to find out what was at the bottom of
Blaney's defiance, and in that time he had heard
no word from his lieutenant. There were but
three days more.

If it were his habit to act on impulse, as his
wonderful quickness led men to believe, he
would have gone straight to Tillman City, and

carried on his fight there in person. But on reflection he concluded that his presence there would be likely to ruin whatever schemes Bridge might be working out. " I'll wait a little longer," he thought.

Bridge was in the hospital. His landlady had found him in his room about an hour after the fever overtook him, and visions of a red quarantine card on her door-post had such disquieting force that in an incredibly short time the doctor and the oldest boarder were carrying the unconscious politician wrapped in a pair of blankets to the carriage which was to take him thither.

Tillman City was proud of its hospital, and the nursing and the medical attention which Bridge received were as good as they could have been. But after all it seemed to make little difference, for the fever raged in him in spite of all efforts to break it. He lay, utterly insensible to his surroundings, the object of the curiosity, as well as the kindness, of those about him; for scarlet fever in a man, especially so severe a case, is enough out of the ordinary to be interesting. Sometimes his delirium became so violent that men had to hold him down to the bed, but for the most of the time he simply rolled and tossed, moaning softly or chattering unintelligible syllables.

Wednesday evening his fever was slightly lower and he lay comparatively quiet. Sitting by the screen which kept the light of the night lamp from his eyes was Grace Burns. She had been a nurse only a little while, and to her Bridge was not a case but a man. She felt a great pity for the pathetic figure on the bed and, when she saw that it was good for him to have her by, she spent more than half the hours of the twenty-four watching him. She was a young woman, not yet thirty, and she had the poise which comes from nerves that are never out of tune. Some of her nervous strength she seemed to impart to him, and he was rarely violent while under her care.

Now as she watched him she saw him throw back the covers and sit up on the edge of the bed. The movement was so quick that before she could reach him he was struggling to his feet.

"The contract," he said. "I must take it to him right away." His voice and his inflection were perfectly natural.

"Yes," she said easily, "I'll attend to that. There's plenty of time. Now lie down again."

He looked at her in a puzzled, questioning way, but obeyed, and in a few moments his moaning told her that the dull fever dreams had again come upon him.

When the doctor came to make his last visit before the night, he looked grave.

"Has he had any lucid intervals?" he asked.

She told him what had happened earlier in the evening.

"It's hard to tell," he said, "whether that was dreams or not."

As he started to go, she asked, —

"Did they tell you downstairs that some one had been here to see him?"

He shook his head.

"He came while I was down in the office, and they said he had been here two or three times before. He wanted to see Mr. Bridge, he said, on a very important business matter."

The doctor smiled. "I'm afraid," he said, "that business will be indefinitely postponed. Who was the man?"

"He's one of our aldermen, Michael Blaney."

They were startled by a cry from the bed. Bridge was sitting bolt upright, and terror was in his face.

"Stop him, Weeks!" he gasped. "He's trying to choke me. Pull him off. You said he shouldn't touch me."

The voice died away in a moan, and he sank back in the pillows, breathing thickly. The nurse slipped quickly to his side, clasped his wrist in her cool hand, and laid the other on his forehead, and in a few moments his breath was coming more regularly and the mad light was gone out of his eyes.

The doctor looked on admiringly. "You'll pull him out of this if anybody can," he said. "It's strange he's got this Weeks business in his head. He hasn't known anything since Sunday night, and there wasn't much about it in the papers up to that time."

There was a silence while the doctor, after a long look at his patient, turned and walked to the door. When he reached it he said: —

"There's something beside scarlet fever that keeps up that delirium, I believe; something on his mind. I'd watch what he says pretty carefully, if I were you. He may give you a clew to

what's bothering him. Then perhaps we can
bring him around. Good night."

Grace Burns was not in the habit of reading
the papers, for her activities, her sympathies,
and her thoughts were pretty well absorbed
without them, but on Thursday morning she
read with eager interest the account of the fight
for the M. & T. railroad. She also read an
editorial on Jim Weeks, and then found out all
she could from the newspapers of the two days
previous. When she had finished, she abandoned a half-formed project of the night before
to write to Weeks and explain the situation to
him on the chance of his being of assistance.
She saw on what a large scale this man did
things and concluded that it was unlikely that
he had any connection with Bridge's affairs, if,
indeed, he had ever heard of him. He would
be too busy to pay much attention to anything
she might write.

All day long she listened to the sick man's
continuous talk, hoping that some meaning
would transpire through the incoherent sentences, something that would guide her to the
source of his trouble; but her patience had
little reward. He spoke vaguely of a contract

x

once or twice, and as many times he mentioned the name of Jim Weeks, and at those times she thought of her plan again; mentally she would begin framing the note she would write to the great capitalist. But as often as she did this she realized that she had nothing to say to him, and with a sigh she put the thought away to wait at least until she could find out something more definite.

The next morning, Friday, she read in the papers of the dramatic happenings of the day before and of Jim Weeks's going to Chicago, presumably for a conference with the Governor. The bigness of it appalled her a little, and again the courage she had been storing up over night to write the note oozed away. For after all it was a question of courage, courage to do something which common sense called absurd on the bare chance that it might do good.

The day was a repetition of the day before, but late in the afternoon the persistent thought, "it might do some good," drove her to write to Jim Weeks. The note read : —

"Mr. Bridge [she did not know his initials] is dangerously sick here in the hospital. He has been delirious ever since he was brought here, and has frequently called for you, sometimes as if he wanted to tell you something, and at others as if he desired your protection. I write in the hope that you will be able either to come or to suggest some clew to his delusions which may enable us to remove them."

It was mailed that evening and reached Jim about noon Saturday. Not half an hour afterward she received a telegram which took a load off her mind : —

Shall reach Tillman at eight this evening and will drive direct to the hospital. Please arrange it so I can see him immediately after I arrive there.

She was in the sick room watching, when Jim was shown in. He walked directly to the bed and stood looking down at Bridge for a moment, and then spoke to Grace Burns.

" Has he any chance? What is it? "

" It's scarlet fever. The doctor doesn't seem to think there's much hope."

" Poor devil," said Jim under his breath.

The nurse suddenly bent forward over the sick man, and motioned Jim to silence. Bridge's lips were moving and he seemed to be struggling to speak.

"Yes, he's here," said the nurse in answer to the half-heard question.

Jim dropped on one knee beside the bed. "Yes, I'm Jim Weeks," he said. " Do you want to tell me anything?"

Again it was the nurse's ear that caught the words, "My coat — in the pocket — the contract."

" I'll get it," she said quickly, and in a moment she had come back into the room, with the coat Bridge had worn when they brought him to the hospital.

Jim took the coat, took a handful of papers out of the pockets and glanced over them. A scrawled and crumpled sheet caught his eye, and straightening it out he read it carefully, holding it close to the dim night lamp. He stood erect again, staring intently at the grotesque shadows on the screen. Grace Burns, who was watching him, saw that for the moment Bridge was forgotten.

But presently his face softened and a smile came into his eyes. Again he went to the bedside and dropped on one knee. He spoke softly, but there was a restrained ring in his voice.

"You've saved us, Bridge; can you understand me? We're going to win out. You were in time."

He took the thin hand that lay on the coverlet and it clasped his convulsively. He looked curiously at the sick man, and then as the weak grip was not relaxed he sat down on the side of the bed and waited. Five minutes crept away, and another five, and then the slow easy breathing told them that Bridge was asleep.

As the hand let go of his, Weeks rose to go. The nurse followed him to the door, where she said simply : —

"Thank you for coming. It saved his life."

"Then it was you who saved it," said Jim. "And you saved me, too. I won't forget it."

CHAPTER XXII

THE WINNING OF THE ROAD

THE Chicago papers reach Tillman City by nine o'clock every morning, and the inhabitants wait till then for information from the outside world. At supper time they read fragmentary Associated Press despatches and a more or less accurate chronicle of local happenings in *The Watchman*. Since the coming of the new editor, Tillman's one daily had contrived to worry along without the assistance of a patent inside, for he was an ambitious young fellow with a knack for writing snappy editorials, and he made the most of the meagre news the city furnished.

He did not hear of Jim's arrival in town and his drive to the hospital until next morning. When told of it, he laid down his pipe and began slipping on his coat.

"I suppose he's in town yet," he said to the reporter who had brought the news. "If he is,

I'm going to see him; then I can make something out of what he might have said. He's the kind that makes me mad. He's got as good a story inside him as any man in the United States this morning, but it would take a chemical process to get it out of him."

Jim was in his room at the Hotel Tremain, trying to decide upon the best way to bring Blaney to terms. The most direct course would be to go to Blaney and try to convince him of the worthlessness of McNally's contract. Blaney was badly scared already: that was evident enough in his manner during the interview Jim had had with him on the artesian road. The two weeks of suspense, during which time it was clear that Jim was winning, would not tend to increase Blaney's confidence. It would not take much of a bluff to complete his demoralization.

But the difficulty lay in the manner of approach. To make the bluff most effective, Blaney should be frightened into seeking Jim. If he went to Blaney's house, the contractor would probably suspect that some weakness in Jim's position made him depend on Blaney's aid. Jim was not worrying over the problem as other men worry, for he had been quite sincere

in telling Bridge that they were sure to win.
Years of this kind of fighting had given him a
just estimate of the immense value of time, and
he had forty-eight hours left in which to get control of the Tillman City stock. Campaigns have
been lost and won again in less time than that.

When the bell-boy brought up the editor's
card Jim stared at it a moment, then told the
boy to show him in. Had the boy looked up
he would have seen that Jim was smiling. His
plan had come to him.

When the editor came into the room he found
Jim lounging in a big chair with his feet on another, bent apparently on spending the morning in luxurious idleness. Jim did not rise but
greeted him cheerfully, and the editor took the
chair Jim nodded to and accepted the cigar Jim
offered him. This was the beginning of what
the editor afterward spoke of as his trance.

For there sat Jim Weeks, the wary, the close-
mouthed, the reporter's despair, artlessly telling
the whole inside history of the fight for the
M. & T.   At first the editor hardly dared
to breathe for fear of bringing Jim to his
senses and the story to a premature conclusion;
but as the President talked apparently in his

right mind, the editor became bolder and began asking questions. In answering, Jim told him that the fight was practically over. It would formally be decided on Tuesday at the stockholders' meeting; but as Jim and his allies controlled a majority of the stock, the outcome was certain.

Then having cleared away the preliminaries Jim came to the point. " Your finance committee here in Tillman is going to vote your stock against us, though," he said. " Porter has pulled their leg with a fake contract, and they're just about big enough fools to be caught by that sort of a game. I've known about it for some time, and I might have done something if we hadn't stood to win anyway. As it is they can't beat us, no matter how they vote."

There were more questions and more perfectly frank answers, and at last the editor knew practically all there was to know about the dealings of the wily Mr. Blaney. Jim did not seem to take the contract very seriously, but he was evidently perfectly familiar with its provisions. When the editor rose to go his head was fairly awhirl.

" Mr. Weeks," he asked, " have you given this story to any one else? "

" No," said Jim.

"We don't come out till to-morrow afternoon," said the editor. "We haven't a Sunday edition. Will the story be any good by that time?"

" That's as you think," said Jim. " I shan't give it to any one else."

The bewildered editor went on his way rejoicing, and Jim packed his bag and started for Chicago. He had planted his mine under Blaney and he could do nothing more with him until the time for exploding it. Jim was satisfied with his plan. The story which *The Watchman* was to print the next afternoon was almost sure to scare Blaney into submission. True, the time was short between the issue of the paper and the stockholders' meeting, but this fact was after all rather to Jim's advantage than otherwise. The only element of uncertainty in Jim's success lay in the possible countermove which McNally might make to reassure Blaney. The chances were, Jim thought, that McNally would not hear of the story in *The Watchman* until Tuesday morning.

Jim reached Chicago late Sunday afternoon.

On Monday he and Harvey were back in the office working on other matters. Not until Tuesday morning did Jim start for Manchester, where the stockholders' meeting was to be held that afternoon.

At eleven o'clock Jim walked into the lobby of the Illinois House, lighted a cigar at the news stand, nodded familiarly to the clerk, and passed on into the writing room. The clerk said to a bell-boy, —

"Go into the bar and tell Mr. Blaney that Jim Weeks is here."

Blaney had been waiting for that message for the past hour, for he had told the clerk to let him know as soon as Jim should arrive, and he had expected him earlier; but now he only swore savagely at the bell-boy, and ordered another whiskey. It was the last of a long series of bracers, and it did its work a little too well.

With soldierly erectness he walked out of the bar, across the lobby, and into the writing room. Jim was writing at a desk and did not look up as Blaney entered, so the contractor went round behind him and dropped his hand heavily on Jim's shoulder.

"I want to talk to you," he said fiercely.

Jim looked up as if to see who it was, and then turned back to his writing.

"Well, talk away," he said.

"I want to see you in private," said Blaney, excited to rage by Jim's indifference.

Jim affected to consider for a moment; then he rose and led the way to the office, where he told the clerk that he wanted a room for an hour or so, and that on no account must he be disturbed.

The two men climbed to the room in silence. When they reached it, Jim followed Blaney in, locked the door behind him, and put the key in his pocket. The action made Blaney nervous, and the warmth at the pit of his stomach was beginning to be succeeded by something that felt like a large lump of cold lead.

"Well," said Jim, "we're private enough now. What have you got to say?"

Blaney pumped up all the bluster he could.

"All I want to find out is, who wrote that story in *The Watchman*."

"That's all, is it?" said Jim. "I could have told you that downstairs. I wrote it."

Then Blaney broke loose. He was working

himself up to a perfect frenzy of denials, accusations, threats, and blasphemy. The man was a pitiable spectacle, and Jim, leaning back against the locked door, watched him in mingled amusement and contempt. He was surprised that Blaney should have become so utterly demoralized. He had never considered the contractor a big man, or even a good fighter, but that he would go to pieces so easily was unexpected. He did not know how violent the explosion in Tillman had been. The town sided with Jim Weeks, and when the people realized how he was to be sold out, the storm exceeded the editor's wildest expectations, and Blaney was brought face to face with political ruin.

Jim let the almost hysterical rage expend itself before he interrupted. Then he said : —

"Shut up, Blaney. You've made a fool of yourself long enough. And I've fooled with you long enough. You've been trying ever since you were alderman to throw me down. You've talked about how much you were going to do, and all the while we've been laughing at you. Then this McNally came along and set up you and Williams to a dinner at the Hotel Tremain and paid you some money and gave you this fool contract, to get you to vote the Tillman City proxies his way."

Jim took a copy of the contract out of his pocket and read it aloud, while Blaney listened in stupid amazement. "McNally is a smart man," Jim went on, folding the contract and replacing it, "and he sized you up just about right when he figured he could take you in with a fake like this, that isn't worth the paper it is written on. And when you'd got fooled so you thought C. & S. C. would pay par for your stock, what do you do but go around and tell a man you know is working for me all about it! And now when I've got you just where I want you, where you can only wriggle, you come around and try to scare me. Do you know what you are? You're just a plain damn fool."

Blaney did not seem to hear the last words of what was probably the longest speech Jim Weeks had ever made. His attention had been riveted on something else.

"Bridge," he exclaimed. "Bridge gave that away, did he?"

"Yes," said Jim; "Bridge gave me this contract. There's just about one more fool thing you can do, Blaney, and that is try to touch him. Try it! Why, man, if you do I'll break you to pieces." The words had a ring in them, but Jim quieted instantly. "I'm looking out for Bridge."

There was a long silence. Blaney dropped limply into a gaudy rocking-chair and with a dirty handkerchief mopped the sweat out of his eyes. Jim had not moved from his position before the door. His lips were grave, but something in his eyes suggested that he was smiling. It was Jim who spoke at last.

"I don't believe you've got anything to say to me, and I haven't much more to say to you. You've got the Tillman proxies for five thousand shares and you're going to vote them in a couple of hours. You can vote them either way you like. It doesn't make much difference to me because I win by at least four thousand even if you go against me. But if you do, you'll find it hard work a year from now to get a city job laying bricks in Tillman. I'll guarantee that. If you choose to vote 'em my way that story in *The Watchman* will fall by its own weight. I'll leave you alone so long as you don't monkey with Bridge."

"I won't monkey with Bridge," said Blaney,

sullenly; "but I'll tell you, you're making a big mistake to take any stock in him. He's been lying to you. I never saw that contract before. He came to me and tried to get me to go up against you, and when I wouldn't he must have got up that contract to get even with me. That's what made me so mad about that story in the papers."

"I see," said Jim, with unshaken gravity. "Well, there's no use in talking any more, I guess. We understand each other." And with these words Jim unlocked the door and walked downstairs to dinner.

By four o'clock it was all over; the road was won, and Jim, struggling into his overcoat, was reflecting on how beautifully success succeeds. For Blaney had not been the only one to change sides, and the result of the election had been a sweeping victory, which surprised even Jim. The stampede had caught Thompson and Wing, and the only holdings which had been voted against him were those directly represented by Porter. Porter had attended the meeting and was surprised to find that his relief at having the fight well over was almost strong enough to make up for his chagrin and disappointment at being defeated.

He met Jim at the door, and after a word of commonplaces he inquired after Harvey.

"He's getting on all right," said Jim. "He got a crack over the head that's bothering him a little, but it's nothing serious."

"Weeks," said Porter, abruptly, "I want a word with you about that affair. That attempt to kidnap him was dirty business. I don't think I need say that it was done without my sanction. The man who was responsible for it is no longer in my employ. Good day."

"That," mused Jim as he drove to the Northern Station, "is what comes of having a daughter like Miss Katherine Porter."

Y

CHAPTER XXIII

THE SURRENDER

JIM looked up from a desk that was piled high with letters and memoranda.

"West, what do think of that?" he said, handing a type-written sheet across to the other desk.

It was an order addressed to Mattison, reinstating J. Donohue in the passenger service of the M. & T.

"He deserves it," replied Harvey, briefly. "Shall I send it on?"

"Yes."

Each turned back to his work. Such interruptions were rare now in Jim's office in the Washington Building. For any man of wide and commanding interests to drop his routine even for a day or so means a busy time catching up later on; and in the case of Jim, who had lost all told the better part of two weeks, the accumulation was almost disheartening, particularly to Harvey.

Although he had to come to Chicago early
Friday morning, spending only one night at the
Oakwood Club, it was not until Monday that
Harvey was able to resume work. In the
meantime he had neither seen nor heard from
Katherine. During that long night at the club
he had planned, in a feverish, restless way, to
drive to her home in the morning; but the
morning saw him speeding to Chicago, weak
and nerveless. During Friday and Saturday
he was confined to his room by order of the
physician, but on Sunday, a bright day, he
walked out.

His first letter to Katherine was written Saturday afternoon. It was a simple statement,
a manly plea for what he desired more than
anything else in the world, and as he read it
over he felt that it must have an effect. That
it deeply moved Katherine was shown by the
reply which came on the following Tuesday.
She did not waste words, but there was in
her little note an honest directness that left
Harvey helpless to reply. She made no con-
cealment of her love, though not stating it,
but repeated practically what she had said that
afternoon at the club. Again it was, " We

must wait — " even indefinitely. Harvey read
the note many times. Tuesday night he sat
down with a wild idea of answering it, but his
inner sense of delicacy restrained him. She
had put the matter in such a light, practically
throwing herself on his generosity, his love
for her, that he realized that to write again
would only make her duty harder. And in
the intervals when Harvey's passionate impatience gave way to calmer reflection, he
knew that he loved her the better for her
strength.

Wednesday and Thursday passed. Harvey's
complete recovery was slow, though he worked
hard at his desk; even the news of Jim's victory seemed to have little effect on him. He
was listless, his work contained little of the
old vigor and energy, and there were rings
under his eyes. Jim said nothing, but he had
not been blind to Katherine's tell-tale interest
when Harvey was found. He knew Harvey,
even better than the younger man suspected.
From the nature of his work and experience
Jim had learned to read human nature, — probably that faculty had much to do with his success, — and the fact that in Harvey's make-up

were certain of his own rugged characteristics had drawn him to Harvey more than to any other man of his acquaintance: this in addition to the one touch of sentiment that had influenced Jim's whole career, for he could not forget that Harvey was the son of the only woman he had ever loved.

Thursday evening Jim sat down to his solitary dinner with a feeling of utter loneliness. There came back to him, clearer than for a quarter of a century, all the yearning, the unrest, the self-abandon of his love for Ethel Harvey. The years had rounded him, and built up in him a sturdy character; he stood before the world a man of solid achievement, calm, successful, satisfied. His spreading interests, his intricate affairs, the prestige and credit of his position — these had combined to concentrate his energies, to hold, day and night, his thoughts, crowding out alike dreams and memories. He had given the best of his life, not for gold, but for power, credit, influence. The struggle had fascinated him, he had risen to each new emergency with a thrill at the thought of grappling with men of mettle, of calling into play each muscle of the system he had organized. But as he left the table and walked with unelastic step into the library, there rose before him the picture of Harvey, weak and pale but filled nevertheless with the vigor of youthful blood, stretched on a couch, while over him, gentle in her womanhood, Katherine was bending. As the scene came back he again moved through it, and again, as he turned to go, he caught a glimpse of her eyes, and he saw in them the look that no man can view without a prayer, a look that melted through the crust of years and left Jim's heart bare.

It was dark in the library, but he cared not. He sat before the wide table staring at the shadows. For the first time in many years he was far from stocks and from the world. He tried madly, desperately, then humbly, to fight down the other picture — that of the only other woman whose eyes had reached his heart; but the struggle was too great, and with head buried on his outstretched arms Jim gave way to a flood burst of memory that poured out years in moments.

Some time later he raised his head. Habits so fixed as Jim's will assert themselves even in moments of stress, and now what was almost an instinct urged him to such action as would even slightly ease the strain. Harvey was his hope, Harvey's happiness and Katherine's was all that appealed to him now, and so with set teeth he rang for his carriage. Jim Weeks had faced many problems, he had gone lightly into many battles, but never before had his energies been so set upon a single object.

Jim drove direct to Harvey's rooms, and, finding them dark, walked in, lighted up, drew down the curtains, and sank wearily into the easy-chair. He was by this time near his old self, save for the wrinkles about his eyes, which seemed deeper. He had not before been in Harvey's quarters, and he looked about with almost nervous interest. Later he picked up the evening paper and tried to read, but dropped it and took to walking about the room. On the mantel was the kodak picture of Katherine, and he paused to look at it. It so held his interest that he did not hear the door open five minutes later.

Harvey closed the door and threw his over-coat on a chair.

"Beg pardon for keeping you waiting," he

said, apparently not surprised at Jim's presence. "If I had known you were here, I'd have come back earlier. Been out for a little exercise."

Jim nodded, and turned back to the photograph.

"This is Porter's daughter, isn't it?" he said abruptly.

With a brief "Yes," Harvey threw himself into a chair by the table. After a moment Jim turned and stood with his back to the mantel, looking at Harvey, then he crossed over and sat down.

"West, I've been thinking of you to-night, and I've come over to have a talk with you. You are in bad shape. You show it plain enough. If it were any other time, if we weren't already so far behind with our work, I'd send you off somewhere for a vacation. You need it."

Harvey smiled wearily.

"A fellow can't expect to get over a row like that in a day or so. I'll be all right in a week."

"Look here," Jim leaned back and looked squarely at Harvey, "why don't you own up?

Why don't you tell me about it? It's — it's her,
isn't it?" indicating the photograph.

Harvey returned Jim's gaze with an expression of some surprise, then he leaned forward
and looked at the carpet, resting his elbows on
his knees.

"Of course," Jim continued, "it isn't exactly
in my line, but I might be able to bring some
common sense to bear on it. When a man's
bothered about a girl, he's likely to need a little
common sense. I understand — of course — if
you'd rather not talk about it —"

There was a long silence. Harvey broke it.

"I don't know but what you're right. I
haven't known just what to do. Things are
pretty much mixed up. You want me to tell
you?"

Jim nodded.

"It isn't that she doesn't care for me. I
think she does. You know she's always
honest. But somehow it strikes her as a
question of duty. She loves her father, and
she feels that she hasn't been loyal to him.
I've written to her, — I've used up all my ar-
guments, — but she puts it in such a way that I
can't say another word without actually hurting

her.   To her mind it's just a plain case of right
and wrong, and that settles it.   You know she's
that kind of a girl."

"Yes," said Jim, " I suppose she is."

" I've gone over and over it until I'm all at
sea.   I don't seem to have a grip on myself.   I
can't write to her or go to see her.   It would
be simply dishonorable after the way she has
talked to me — and written."   Harvey rose and
walked to the mantel, resting his elbows on it
and looking at the photograph.

"When was it?" asked Jim.   "That day in
the Oakwood Club?"

"Yes."

" And you know she loves you?"

" I didn't say I knew it."

"Well, then, I do."

At this Harvey turned, but Jim's face was
quiet.

"Yes, I know it.   You say there is nothing
in the way but her father?"

"That is all I know about."

"I can ease your mind on that.   I had a short
talk with Porter Tuesday, and I think he's
a little ashamed of himself.   He told me that
he was against that kidnapping scheme and

that he has broken with McNally. Probably Miss Porter has had a talk with him by this time, — I don't see how they could help it, — and if she has, I guess some of her ideas have changed a little."

Jim paused, but as Harvey stood facing the mantel without speaking he went on : —

" There's just one thing for you to do, West. You go down there and begin all over again. If she's got any pride, she won't write to you — Why, man, any girl would expect — You've got to! Understand? You've got to!"

As he spoke Jim rose and stood erect; then, as Harvey still was silent, he took to pacing the floor. Harvey was looking, not at the picture, but through it into a calm summer night on the river, when Katherine had given him that first glimpse of herself, the woman he loved and was always to love. He saw her beside him in the trap, watching with bright, eager eyes the striding bays, and later tugging at his watch-fob. He saw her in the gray twilight, bending down over him and saying in that low thrilling voice: " We don't know what may happen. We only know what is right for us now." As he slowly turned around he felt a mist come over his eyes and he was not ashamed. Jim stopped and stood looking at him. Harvey asked simply, —

"Can you spare me over Sunday?"

"You'd better go to-morrow."

"But the work?"

"I don't want to hear about that," — Jim's voice was gruff, — "you take the morning train. Don't come back till you're ready."

Their eyes met in embarrassed silence, then Harvey sat at the table and wrote a few words.

"Will you have your man send that to-night?" he asked, handing it to Jim. "It's a telegram."

Jim took it, slowly folded it, and put it into his pocket. He reached for his coat, and Harvey helped him put it on. Several times Jim started to speak, but it was not until one glove was on and his hat in his hand that he got it out : —

"I'll tell you, West, I — A man learns something from experience, one way or another. I've known what such things are — I know what it means to love a woman, and to try to live without her." He suddenly gripped Harvey's hand, holding it for a moment with a silent, nervous pressure, and Harvey felt the perspiration on his palm. "I made a mistake, West, and I've paid for it — I'm paying for it now. If I hadn't — If I had made it right, she would have been — you would have — " The words seemed to choke him, and with a strange expression he loosened his grip and started toward the door. Halfway he turned. As he stood there, stalwart yet humble, a new pathos crept into his features. "West, a man doesn't get much in this world if he waits for things to straighten themselves out. Good night."

Before Harvey could recover from a certain awkwardness, Jim had gone. He could hear the heavy tread on the stairs. Then came the slam of a carriage door, and he knew that Jim was going back to the big, empty house.

The next morning, Friday, Harvey took the early train for Truesdale. He picked up a carriage at the station and drove rapidly out to Porter's home. From the porte-cochère he hastened to the door, rang the bell, and asked for her. In the wide hall he stood, coat still buttoned, hat in hand, looking eagerly up the stairway. In a moment she appeared (he could not know that she had been watching for him), coming slowly down the stairs, not hesitating, but holding back with a touch of the old dignity. For the moment her beauty, her strong womanhood, gave Harvey a sense of awe, and he stood looking up at her, not knowing that his eyes told the story. And then, as she stayed on the lower step, a quiet assertiveness came over him, and he stepped forward.

"Katherine," he said, and extended both hands.

She still hesitated, looking at him with eyes that seemed to question, to read his as if searching for something she feared might not be there; then she took the last step and stood before him.

"Katherine," he repeated, but stopped again, for now her eyes were shining on him with a look that thrilled and exalted him, and with sudden joy in his heart he drew her to him.